A bullet slammed into the window. Right next to Linnea's head.

Jace saw the safety glass crack into a spiderweb, but it held in place. The bullet didn't get through. But a second one tore into those cracks, weakening the glass even more.

Gulping in some hard breaths, he fought to clear his vision. Fought, too, to figure out where the hell the shooter was.

"Just stay down," Jace ordered.

But the next bullet ripped through the window, leaving a fist-sized hole and showering Linnea and him with safety glass.

Determined to stop this SOB, he looked through the front windshield to the area where he was sure the shots were coming from. And he saw something.

Or rather *someone*.

A man wearing a ski mask.

Since the windshield was bullet resistant, it wouldn't do Jace any good to return fire through it, and Linnea was in the way for him to get a good shot through the damaged window. Still, it would have to do.

He lifted his gun. Took aim. And he fired.

PURSUED BY THE SHERIFF

USA TODAY Bestselling Author

DELORES FOSSEN

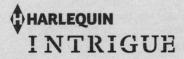

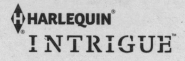

Recycling programs for this product may not exist in your area.

ISBN-13: 978-1-335-48931-9

Pursued by the Sheriff

Copyright © 2021 by Delores Fossen

This edition published by arrangement with Harlequin Books S.A.

For questions and comments about the quality of this book, please contact us at CustomerService@Harlequin.com.

Harlequin Enterprises ULC
22 Adelaide St. West, 41st Floor
Toronto, Ontario M5H 4E3, Canada
www.Harlequin.com

Printed in U.S.A.

Delores Fossen, a *USA TODAY* bestselling author, has written over one hundred novels, with millions of copies of her books in print worldwide. She's received a Booksellers' Best Award and an RT Reviewers' Choice Best Book Award. She was also a finalist for a prestigious RITA® Award. You can contact the author through her website at www.deloresfossen.com.

Books by Delores Fossen

Harlequin Intrigue

Mercy Ridge Lawmen

Her Child to Protect
Safeguarding the Surrogate
Targeting the Deputy
Pursued by the Sheriff

Longview Ridge Ranch

Safety Breach
A Threat to His Family
Settling an Old Score
His Brand of Justice

The Lawmen of McCall Canyon

Cowboy Above the Law
Finger on the Trigger
Lawman with a Cause
Under the Cowboy's Protection

HQN

Last Ride, Texas

Spring at Saddle Run
Christmas at Colts Creek

Visit the Author Profile page at Harlequin.com.

CAST OF CHARACTERS

Sheriff Jace Castillo—His investigation into a dirty cop puts him and everyone around him in extreme danger. That includes the dirty cop's sister, Linnea, but Jace vows to keep her alive no matter the cost.

Linnea Martell—Her brother is on the run from the law and wants her dead so she has no choice but to turn to Jace. Their past could turn out to be a deadly distraction.

Gideon Martell—A San Antonio cop linked to a crime ring that's stealing and selling confiscated goods. He's tying up loose ends by eliminating anyone who's onto him, but it's possible that Gideon's not working alone.

Lt. Bryce Cannon—Gideon's boss in the San Antonio Police Department. He's a powerful cop who might have misused his power, and he could be part of Gideon's crime ring.

Lionel Zimmerman—The ATF agent insists on being the one to bring in Gideon, but he could have ulterior motives.

Tammy Wheatly—A criminal informant who's caught up in the investigation into Gideon's criminal activity. But does she know more than she's saying?

Chapter One

A jab of lightning sliced through the night sky, and Sheriff Jace Castillo caught a glimpse of the man he was chasing—just as the bullet from the guy's semiautomatic slammed into Jace's left shoulder.

The pain was instant and raw. A searing jolt of fire knifed through him, but Jace managed to scramble into a cluster of trees.

It was too dark for Jace to see the wound, but it was already throbbing. And bleeding. He was losing way too much blood. He could feel the warmth of it spreading across the front of his shirt and his sleeve.

Jace looked out into the curtain of rain, the fat drops dripping off the low-hanging tree branch that he was using for cover. He couldn't see the man who'd just shot him, but Jace knew he was still there. Detective Gideon Martell likely wouldn't just walk away from this. Or turn himself in.

Because Gideon was a dirty cop.

Jace had proof of that, and that was why he'd come to Gideon's rural house just outside of Culver Crossing—the town where Jace was the sheriff. He'd intended to arrest Gideon and take him to San Antonio, where Gideon was a decorated officer.

And where they'd been friends, once.

"You still alive, *Sheriff*?" Gideon called out. He said Jace's title as if he didn't have much respect for it. Of course, as Jace had recently learned, Gideon didn't have any respect for his own badge. "It was real stupid of you to come to my place without backup."

Yeah, it had been, but Jace had thought he could talk Gideon into surrendering. So much for that plan. Gideon had run. Jace had gone in pursuit. Now, he'd been shot, and they were deep in the woods, a little more than half mile from the road. Despite the darkness and the storm, Gideon had managed a good run so he could escape.

"You don't want to add murder to your sheet," Jace threw out there, and he moved as fast as he could, darting to the side.

Good thing, too, because Gideon sent a bullet toward the exact spot where Jace had just been. The storm obviously hadn't affected Gideon's hearing or vision, because he had managed to pinpoint Jace's location.

Wincing at the movement and listening for any sound that Gideon was coming closer, Jace took out his phone to call for backup. And he cursed. No signal. There were plenty of dead spots like that in rural Texas, but this was one dead spot that could be fatal for him. He wasn't sure he could make it all the way back to his truck. Especially since he was already starting to get dizzy from the pain and the blood loss.

"My guess is you're hurting pretty bad right now, huh?" Gideon called out.

Again, Jace heard the taunt in his tone and figured the detective was hoping he'd answer. Then Gideon could try to shoot him again, this time with a kill shot.

Too bad about that, on several levels.

It was bad enough that his former best friend wanted him dead, but it also meant he wouldn't be able to talk to Gideon, to try to get answers that he desperately needed.

Answers as to why Gideon had sullied his badge by stealing and then selling confiscated weapons and drugs.

Heaven knew how long Gideon had gotten away with his crimes, but he'd sold the illegal goods to the wrong man. One who'd not only reported it to Jace but had also given him the proof to back it up.

Dragging in a hard breath, Jace put away his phone and focused. He needed to turn this situation around. Needed to figure out Gideon's location so he could end this before he passed out and died here.

"What about Linnea?" Jace asked a split second before he moved again. As expected, Gideon fired a shot and, thankfully, missed this time. "Have you thought about what this will do to her?"

Silence. And Jace hoped it was a good strategy, to use Gideon's sister to make him rethink this. Gideon and Linnea were close, and it would tear out Linnea's heart to know what her brother had done.

"To hell with Linnea," Gideon snarled. "She's the one who ratted me out."

Everything inside Jace went still. He hadn't known that. And he wasn't even sure it was true. Jace certainly hadn't gotten any proof of his wrongdoing from Gideon's sister.

"As far as I'm concerned, Linnea can die right along with you," Gideon added in a snap.

Jace pushed aside those hard words, and he knew it was now or never. He darted out from cover, took aim at the sound of Gideon's voice and fired. Not once but three times. Jace heard the sound of a bullet ripping through flesh. Heard Gideon's sharp groan of pain.

Then he caught a glimpse of his former friend collapsing onto the ground.

Jace's stomach clenched over the thought that he'd likely just killed a man. But he worried even more over another possibility. That he *hadn't* killed Gideon. That Gideon could get up and finish him off.

Because he had no choice, Jace caught onto the tree, using it to anchor himself. The rough bark dug into his hands, but his grip stopped him from falling. For now anyway. Jace could feel himself losing it, though. Losing the battle to stay on his feet, or even to remain just conscious.

The dizziness came with a vengeance. So did the pain. Like hot pokers jabbing at him. Mercy, there was no way he could walk out of this.

He gulped in his breath, and even though he tried to keep holding on, he found himself unable to. He fell, his head smacking against a sharp rock. More pain, but he didn't have enough breath to do anything other than groan.

Jace saw another jab of lightning. Right before everything turned dark.

Chapter Two

With the shotgun gripped in her hand, Linnea Martell stood at the window and kept watch.

It was still storming, the rain and angry wind battering against the tin roof of the tiny log cabin, but it was now thankfully light enough that she could see the small clearing and the woods beyond it. Of course, even with daybreak she might not be able to see the danger before it was too late.

Heck, it could already be too late.

Forcing back that thought, Linnea glanced over her shoulder when she heard the moan. It wasn't a surprising sound. Jace had been doing a lot of moaning since she'd brought him here about six hours ago.

Even though she didn't have any lights on in the cabin and the bed was tucked at an angle deep into the corner, she could see that he was way too pale from the blood loss and the head injury. Also, even in sleep he was likely in pain from the makeshift nursing job she'd done on his shoulder.

She prayed she'd done the right thing.

It occurred to her that she'd never seen him in bed, much less weak and hurting. Linnea had known him since they were kids, and once they'd been as thick as thieves along with her brother, Gideon. She was betting there'd be no such *thickness* now. In fact, it was possible that Jace might want to arrest her for what she'd done.

He moaned again, turning his head from side to side, as if to ward off some nightmare. Or the pain he had to be feeling. His midnight-black hair brushed against the stark white pillowcase, and his forehead bunched up. Since he'd also been doing that a lot ever since he'd been in her cabin, Linnea figured he would just drift back off. His body needed the rest.

But his eyes opened.

Even though she couldn't see the color of them from where she stood, she knew they were a deep, smoky gray. Cop's eyes. But once they'd caused her heart to jitter in a different kind of way, when she'd had a crush on him. Maybe she still did, but it wasn't a crush she was feeling right now.

"Where am I?" Jace mumbled. Wincing and grunting, he tried to sit up, but Linnea hurried to him to ease him back down.

"Don't move," she warned him. "You'll start bleeding again."

He blinked, then stared at her. "Linnea?" It was enough of a question to make her think that his vision was blurry. But the blur was better than his being unconscious.

"Yes." She kept her voice soft and as reassuring as she could manage, which probably wasn't very effective, considering she was holding a shotgun.

And Jace noticed that, too.

His gaze drifted from her face to the gun and then around the cabin. Since the place was only about eight hundred square feet, there wasn't a lot of it to take in.

With his breath gusting, Jace stayed quiet several long moments, clearly trying to process everything, and then he cursed when he looked down at the bandage. Linnea had wrapped it around his chest, anchoring his arm to his side so that he couldn't move it too much while he'd been unconscious.

"Gideon," Jace muttered.

He groaned, squeezed his eyes shut a moment and cursed some more. It was like profanity stew, the words running together in a jumbled heap.

"Gideon's dirty," he finally managed to get out. "He's the one who shot me."

"Yes, I know," Linnea whispered.

She didn't hesitate with her response, but just admitting it out loud felt as if someone had clamped a fist around her heart. Sweet heaven, this hurt. It hurt more than anything she'd ever felt—including when her parents had died. Probably because that'd happened in a car accident. But what Gideon had done was on purpose.

"Gideon doctored chain-of-evidence records," Linnea continued a moment later. "He took guns and drugs from evidence stored at a San Antonio PD warehouse, and he sold them."

Jace went quiet again. Then he nodded. "*To hell with Linnea. She's the one who ratted me out.* That's what Gideon said to me right before he shot me." Something flickered through his eyes, and he tried to get up again. He managed to sit up even though he went sheet-white, and grimaced from the pain. "I shot him. I think I killed him."

Linnea glanced quickly out the window and then looked Jace straight in the eyes. "No, you didn't. I mean, yes, you shot him. At least I think you did. But he's not dead. I looked for his body, and I didn't find it."

That had caused her to feel a flood of relief.

And dread.

Gideon wasn't dead. Or at least he hadn't died in or near the spot where he'd likely been shot—which would have been fairly close to where she'd found Jace. That meant Gideon had managed to move, to get out of the area without leaving any trace of himself behind. But depending on his injury, he could have collapsed elsewhere. Or he could have escaped and gone on the run. Sadly, that last one was the best-case scenario for Jace and her.

She watched as Jace tried to process what she'd just told him, and the muscles in his jaw stirred against each other. "What happened? How'd I get here? And where the hell is Gideon?"

All reasonable questions for a man who'd been shot and then unconscious for hours. Since this wasn't going to be short and sweet, Linnea went back to the window to keep watch.

"I don't know where Gideon is," she said. "But he could be close by. That's why I've been keeping watch."

Jace glanced around again. "Where are we? Where is this place?"

"We're about ten miles from Culver Crossing. This cabin belonged to my grandparents, but I inherited it. I came here after I found out what Gideon had been doing."

It probably wasn't smart to come to a location that Gideon knew about, but she hadn't wanted to go to her house or her office, both of which were in Culver Crossing, and she hadn't had enough cash to go to a hotel in a nearby city. Linnea had been a cop's sister long enough to know that if she used her credit card, Gideon would be able to trace it.

And find her.

"Before I came here, I went to his house, confronted him, and…" Linnea had to stop, gather her breath and tamp down her heartbeat, which was starting to race. "He told me to mind my own business. He said that if I truly loved him, I'd forget what I'd learned about him."

"He threatened you," Jace concluded after several long moments.

There went that fist around her heart again. It tightened like a vise. "I think he would have, but before he could threaten or try to intimidate me, someone came to the door. A man. I don't know who he was, but while they were talking—arguing, really—I slipped out Gideon's back door, ran to my car, jumped in and drove off."

But she hadn't just left. Linnea had sped away, getting out of there as fast as she could. She'd caught a glimpse of her brother in her rearview mirror, and what she'd seen on his face had turned her blood to ice. There hadn't been a trace of the love that'd once been between them.

"Did Gideon follow you?" Jace asked. He was sounding more like a cop now, trying to get to the truth.

She shook her head. "But that probably would have been his next move if I hadn't turned onto a side road and hid between two buildings. Then I called his boss, Lieutenant Bryce Cannon, at San Antonio PD, and I told him everything. Lieutenant Cannon said they'd send someone out to pick up Gideon, so I came here. To hide out. To try to make some sense of why my brother had done this."

It'd been hours now, and she still hadn't made

sense of it. Linnea knew there was the possibility that she never would.

"Why'd you go back to Gideon's?" he asked. "Because I'm guessing that's where you were when you found me."

She nodded. "I wasn't going to confront him, but I wanted to see if he was still there. Or try to figure out where he'd gone so I could tell his lieutenant. I knew as long as Gideon was out there, that someone could be hurt."

And she'd been right about that.

"Anyway, I walked through the woods from here to get to Gideon's house," she continued. "It's about a mile and a half away on the trails. I was still on one of those trails when I heard the shots being fired. I didn't know what was going on, but then I found you."

She'd been terrified that he was dead. Then, when she'd realized Jace was alive, her first priority had been to keep him alive.

"If Gideon's injuries aren't that serious, he'll come here," Linnea said.

"To finish us off," Jace added.

Linnea didn't want to believe Gideon would kill them. But her brother was desperate, and since he'd already tried to murder Jace, it wasn't a stretch to believe he'd try again.

Cursing again, Jace threw off the cover and managed to swing his legs off the bed. The sheet stayed over the lower half of his body, but his face became masked with a fine mist of sweat and pain.

"You really should lie down," she warned him. "It took some doing to get the bleeding to stop. You were lucky that the bullet went clean through." Though she doubted he was feeling particularly lucky at the moment.

Jace didn't lie down, but he didn't try to get up, either. His gaze skimmed his bare chest and his clothes that were draped over a chair at the foot of the bed.

"You were soaking wet when I got you here," she explained. "There's a washer and dryer, so I stripped off your clothes and dried them."

He glanced down at the sheet then and obviously didn't have any trouble figuring out that he was butt naked. Jace gave a soft grunt, as if to dismiss any qualms over that, and lightly touched his fingers to the lump and bruise on his forehead.

"You tended to me?" he asked. "You put this bandage on me?"

She nodded. "There was a medical book with the first aid kit in the storage cabinet. It didn't say how to treat a gunshot, but I followed the instructions on a deep puncture wound. I don't think I screwed it up, but there wasn't anything I could do about the head injury. For that, you need tests done at a hospital."

He mumbled what she thought might be a thank-you. "How'd I get here?"

Not easily, but Linnea gave him the condensed version. "After I found you shot, I came back here for the ATV that was in the shed." Thankfully, the shed had been big enough for her to put her car inside so that anyone coming near the cabin wouldn't immediately see it. "I managed to get you on the ATV, and I brought you here."

Again, Jace stayed quiet a moment, obviously trying to process what she'd told him. "We need to call for backup," he insisted.

Linnea knew he wasn't going to like this. "There's no signal out here, so the phones don't work. There isn't any internet, either, so I can't email anyone."

Jace groaned, shook his head, and she could see the frustration on his face that was no doubt on hers. The rest of what she had to tell him wouldn't help.

"The storm washed the road out, so we can't leave in my car. How far away are you parked?" she asked. Though it would be a challenge to get Jace anywhere right now—especially if Gideon was out there, waiting to gun them down.

He considered it a moment, repeated the headshake. "Not close enough. We can get out with the ATV."

Linnea had already given this plenty of thought. And dismissed using it. "It's still storming, and any movement could cause you to start bleeding again. I couldn't do stitches, so basically I've just bandaged you together with what I found in the first aid kit."

At least there'd been some antiseptic salve and even gauze to pack the wound, but everything she'd done was just a temporary fix.

"I'll be okay," he grunted. But when he tried to stand up, he groaned in pain and dropped back down onto the bed.

"There's ibuprofen," Linnea offered. She tipped her head to the bottle and the glass of water she'd put on the nightstand for him. They were next to his holster, gun and phone. "Sorry, but I don't have anything stronger."

With his hands a little unsteady, he opened the bottle and downed several of the pills. With even more unsteadiness, Jace stood while he tried to keep the sheet in place over his groin. When he wobbled, catching onto the headboard of the bed, Linnea hurried to him, propping the shotgun against the wall so she could slip her arm around him.

It was a bad time for her to notice how his bare skin felt. Warm and all man. *Naked*. Yes, a stupid time. Then again, she often had stupid thoughts when it came to Jace.

"Are you okay?" he asked.

That got her attention, and her gaze whipped up to his.

"You made a weird sound," Jace added.

Oh, that. Probably a sigh that went with the dopey thoughts of having him stripped bare and so close to her.

"Knee-jerk reaction," she said, trying to keep her voice level and light. "It's from all those years of making sure we didn't end up near a bed together."

The corner of his mouth lifted, and despite his pain-ravaged eyes, he still managed to look, well, incredibly hot. That was Jace. And she hadn't lied when she'd said they made an art form of avoiding each other.

His smile vanished. "Because of Gideon," he muttered.

Yes. It had been her brother's insistence that Jace keep his hands off her. In part because she was four years younger than the two of them. Also in part because Gideon didn't want his best friend *messing around* with his kid sister. Even though it had never made a lot of sense to Linnea, it clearly had gotten through to Jace, since he'd honored Gideon's demand.

Well, except for that one kiss.

It had happened a little over a decade ago, on her eighteenth birthday. A kiss that Jace had likely meant to be just a friendly peck when he'd found her in Gideon's barn while she was saddling one of the horses. But it had turned as scalding hot as he was. It had also ended when Jace had come to his senses and stepped back.

Way back.

And he'd never stepped toward her again.

Because that kiss, and the memory of it, always

fuzzed her mind, Linnea pushed it aside and focused on the Texas-sized problems that were facing Jace and her.

"I need to keep watch," she reminded him. "Let me help you get into your boxers and jeans."

That, of course, meant seeing him in the buff again. When she'd taken off his clothes, she hadn't even thought about it. Linnea had been too scared that he might die. And he'd been unconscious. Well, he was alert now, and his gaze connected with hers as she brought over his clothes.

Once she had his feet and legs into his boxers and jeans, Linnea helped him up so she could shimmy the items up and in place. She zipped him and got more memories. Fantasies about unzipping him. She clamped her teeth over her bottom lip so that she didn't make that weird sound again.

Even though she didn't especially want him walking around, Linnea helped with his socks and boots when Jace reached for them.

"You can't wear the shirt," she said. "Well, not without me rebandaging you. I'd rather not do that, not until the wound's had some more time to close up."

He didn't argue with her about that. Jace was already back in cop mode, glancing around the room, and his attention soon landed on the keypad next to the front door.

"You have a security system," Jace said. "Will it alert a security company or the cops if it goes off?"

Good question. And it was one she'd already considered. "No. Basically, it's just a loud alarm meant to scare off any would-be burglars. Other than the guns and the ATV, there isn't much to steal around here, and the guns were in a hidden safe built into the floor."

Linnea made sure he was steady enough to stand alone, and picking up the shotgun, went back to the window. She turned and scanned the woods again. Nothing. But the wind had picked up, and it was tossing the branches around as the rain continued to batter the window. The whipping motion of the oaks and cedars would make it harder to see Gideon.

"I think the best plan is for me to take the ATV and go to Culver Crossing," she said. "But I can't do that until the lightning stops. Or until you can keep watch without keeling over."

When Jace didn't say anything, she turned to him and saw that he was giving her a seriously skeptical look. "You're a landscape designer," he pointed out. "You've got no training that can help if you were to meet Gideon along the way."

Linnea huffed. Not because she was dismissing what he'd said. It was true she had no firearms training, which was why she was holding a shotgun instead of the handgun she'd found in the floorboard lockbox. It would be easier to hit a target with a shotgun.

If she could hit it, that is.

She knew it wouldn't be easy to aim a gun at her brother and pull the trigger, but she couldn't just stand by and let Gideon kill Jace and her.

"Plus, if the road's out," Jace went on, "the ATV could get stuck."

"I'm strong," she pointed out. "All that dragging around plants, rocks and mulch have given me a few muscles. I managed to get you on the ATV."

Best not to point out, though, that it had been plenty hard, and there'd been moments where she hadn't been sure she could do it.

"If need be, I could run my way out of these woods. You can't run," Linnea added.

"No, but I can return fire if we get into trouble," Jace argued. "And I stand a better chance of hitting a target than you do."

It was a good argument. Well, it would have been if he hadn't had the gunshot wound. It wasn't on his shooting arm, thank goodness, but he was weak, and any movement could cause that wound to open up.

"You could bleed out before I get you out of these woods," Linnea reminded him. "Besides, I'm not sure you can shoot, much less shoot straight. You can't even stand up without help."

As if to prove her wrong, he picked up his gun

from the nightstand and straightened his posture, pulling back his shoulders.

And what little color he had drained from his face.

Cursing him and their situation, she dragged a chair closer to the window and had him sit down.

"The main road isn't that far, only about a mile," she continued. Linnea tried to tamp down her argumentative tone. "I can get there on the ATV and call for help. Your deputies and the EMTs can figure out the best way to get you to a hospital."

That was the part of her plan that worked. What she didn't feel comfortable about was leaving Jace alone while she got to the main road. Definitely not ideal, but they didn't have any other workable solutions.

Of course, this option wouldn't work until the lightning stopped. She could get through the wind and rain, but if she got struck by lightning or a tree falling from a strike, it could be fatal. First, to her, and then to Jace, since he'd be stuck here in the cabin.

He looked up at her, his color a little better now, and his eyes were hard and intense. "I can't let you take a risk like that. Gideon could ambush you."

"That's true," she admitted. "But the alternative is for us to wait here. Maybe for days until you're strong enough to ride out with me. That might not be wise since I suspect you need antibiotics for your wound before an infection starts brewing."

His jaw tightened, and even though he'd had plenty trouble standing, Jace got up. This time he didn't stagger, but she did notice the white-knuckle grip he had on his gun. "We'll see how I feel once the storm has passed."

In other words, he would insist on going with her. Linnea sighed. Obviously, Jace had a mile-wide stubborn streak and was planning on dismissing her *one workable option*.

"If you're hungry, there's some canned soup in the cabinet," she said, shifting the subject.

Jace didn't respond to that. However, he did step in front of her as if to shield her. And he lifted his gun.

"Get down," Jace ordered. "Someone's out there."

Chapter Three

Jace forced back the pain so he could focus. He'd seen some movement in the trees behind the cabin, and he figured it was too much to hope that it was a deer or some other animal. Yes, he'd shot Gideon, but that didn't mean his former friend hadn't made his way here to permanently silence Linnea and him.

"I don't see anything," Linnea said, her breath already too fast.

Obviously, she'd ignored his order for her to get down. An order that had been more cop training than the smart thing to do. If Gideon was truly out there, Jace might have to rely on Linnea's help. Again. She'd likely saved his life by bringing him to the cabin, and now he would need her for backup.

Blinking hard to clear his eyes, he tried to pick through the dense clutter of the trees and underbrush. Nothing. But he kept watching. Kept his gun ready, too.

And then he saw it.

Or, rather, saw *him*.

A man. He was wearing a dark green rain parka, and he was peering out from the trees, his attention aimed at the cabin. Jace's body jolted with the slam of adrenaline. He braced for the fight.

"That's not Gideon," Jace muttered, and he used his hip to nudge Linnea to the side so that she wasn't directly in front of the window.

"No. I think it's the man who came to see him," Linnea explained. "The one who showed up shortly after I confronted Gideon at his place."

Jace kept his gaze nailed to the guy. He wasn't moving, but with that bulky parka, it was impossible to tell if he was armed. "You don't know who he is?"

She shook her head, causing her sandy-brown ponytail to swish. "But like I said, he was arguing with Gideon."

So this could be one of Gideon's partners in crime. Jace figured there had to be at least one person who'd aided Linnea's brother with getting those crates of guns and cases of drugs from evidence storage. Or maybe Gideon's visitor had even been the one in charge of the plan that had netted Gideon a small fortune. It was possible this guy had been in on that fortune-making and had come here to help his partner cover up their crimes.

But Jace rethought that.

"You said you'd called Gideon's lieutenant at SAPD?" he asked Linnea.

She nodded and kept her attention on the man.

"Lieutenant Bryce Cannon. But I know Cannon, and that's not him outside."

No, but it could be someone sent by Cannon. And that wouldn't be good, if the lieutenant was as dirty as Gideon. If so, then killing Linnea and him would go a long way to hiding their crimes.

"Crimes," Jace muttered under his breath. The throbbing pain in his shoulder and head cleared enough for him to realize he should have already thought of something. "Toby."

Linnea gave him a confused glance. "Toby Conway?" she asked.

"Yeah," Jace verified.

Linnea knew him, of course. Most folks in and around Culver Crossing did because Toby had been in trouble with the law for pretty much all his life. In fact, Jace had arrested him for breaking and entering. For drug possession, too. But other than a short stint in jail for the B and E, Toby hadn't seen too much of the inside of a cage.

"Toby came to me," Jace continued. The man outside moved just a fraction, causing Jace to pause. But the guy didn't come an inch closer to the cabin. Nor did he aim a weapon in their direction. "Toby had a recording of Gideon offering him a piece of the action in the illegal gun racket. Gideon was sure Toby would be interested in something like that."

"But he wasn't?" Linnea asked.

"No. In fact, Toby was scared when he came to

me. He'd let Gideon believe he would take part in the gunrunning, but Toby had no intention of getting involved. Not in something that serious. That means Gideon could go after him to make sure he stays silent about the offer."

Linnea's quick breath let him know that she'd followed that through to a possible bad conclusion. Gideon could murder Toby. In fact, that could be happening right now while Linnea and he stood around, waiting for the guy in the parka to do something. They'd already wasted precious minutes that they might need to save Toby and anyone else in Gideon's or this man's paths.

"Keep back," Jace instructed, and he reached out to lift the window a fraction. Pain shot through him as fast and hard as a bullet, and he had no choice but to stagger back. "I want to call out to him," Jace managed to say.

Huffing, Linnea volleyed glances at him and the man, obviously trying to figure out if that was a stupid idea. Apparently, she decided to side with Jace because she shifted the shotgun enough so that she could unlock the window. The moment she lifted it, the alarm went off.

Linnea cursed, but her words were drowned out by the deafening sound. She had been right about the security system making a loud noise. It blared through the cabin, no doubt through the woods, too. It certainly got the man's attention, but he didn't run.

He came closer.

Linnea hurried to the security panel by the front door, turned off the system to silence it and ran back to the window. "Sorry, I forgot about the alarm."

Jace didn't mind. The alarm turned out to be just as effective as his shouting would have been.

"Gideon Martell?" the man yelled before Jace could say anything. "Are you in there? Is Linnea with you? I want to make sure she's all right."

It was hard to tell if their visitor was actually concerned about Linnea or if he was just trying to home in on a target.

"Get down," Jace told her. He'd needed her help to get the window open, but he wanted to handle the rest of this while she was out of target range.

Linnea gave Jace a quick glare, but she got down. Sort of. She crouched lower but stayed right by the window.

"I'm Jace Castillo, Sheriff of Culver Crossing," Jace yelled. "Who the hell are you, and what do you want?"

Because Jace kept his attention on the man, he saw the guy's posture relax a little. "ATF Special Agent Lionel Zimmerman. I'm going to reach under this rain gear and get my badge."

Again, Jace watched as Zimmerman brought out his badge and held it up. Of course, Jace couldn't get a good look at it from this distance, but it appeared to be a gold badge from the Bureau of Alcohol, Tobacco, Firearms and Explosives.

Appeared to be.

Jace wasn't just going to trust this guy based on what might or might not be real credentials.

"What do you want?" Jace repeated.

"I need to make sure Linnea Martell is all right," Zimmerman answered without hesitation. "Is she with you? Is Gideon here?"

Jace ignored the agent's questions and went with two of his own. "Why do you want to check on Linnea? How do you know her?"

Zimmerman wasn't so quick to answer this time. "I don't know her personally, but I know her brother." He paused. "Gideon's in a lot of trouble, and I'm worried he might have tried to hurt his sister."

Not yet, but Gideon had sure as hell tried to *hurt* Jace. "What kind of trouble is Gideon in?" Jace pressed, fishing for as much info as he could get from this guy.

Every little bit might help Jace figure out if Zimmerman was who he was claiming to be. Too bad they didn't have a working phone or internet so he could do a quick run on this guy.

Zimmerman muttered some profanity. "Why don't I come in so we can talk? I'd rather not discuss this while standing out in the rain, and I really do need to make sure Linnea is all right. Tell me if Gideon and she are with you."

Jace debated what to say. One thing was for certain—Zimmerman wasn't getting inside until Jace was sure he was indeed a federal agent, one who wasn't swimming in the same dirty water as Gideon.

"Explain to me about Gideon's trouble," Jace repeated. "Then you convince me that you're here to help, not hurt."

Even with the distance between them, it wasn't hard to tell that Zimmerman wasn't pleased about that. "Gideon's been selling items confiscated during busts and arrests conducted by the San Antonio PD and the Texas Rangers. The Bureau has reason to believe that he's now on the run and will try to eliminate anyone who might have proof or knowledge of his wrongdoing."

That meshed with Jace's theory. "Does that mean Gideon's trying to eliminate you?" Jace fired back.

"Yes. And you." Zimmerman paused again. "We've had Gideon's place under camera surveillance. We saw the feed when you went to his place to confront him. We saw him run, and you went in pursuit."

Jace wanted to know if Zimmerman had also seen him get shot. Or if he'd seen Jace shoot Gideon. But Jace didn't want to give Zimmerman those sort of details.

"Since you knew I was in trouble, it would have

been nice if you'd sent me some backup," Jace responded.

"We did. Obviously, it took a while to get out to Gideon's place, and I started a search of the area where I last saw the two of you. I've been looking for both of you." Zimmerman paused again. "I'm guessing Gideon's not with you. Where is he?"

That was the million-dollar question, and if Zimmerman was being straight with them, then it meant he hadn't found Gideon's body.

"Gideon's not here," Jace finally said. "I don't know where he is. And yeah, he tried to kill me."

"What about his sister?" Zimmerman quickly asked. "Did Gideon try to kill her, too?"

"Not yet. But I suspect that's because he hasn't gotten the chance. You're not going to have a chance to do that, either," Jace warned him.

Zimmerman nodded, and it looked as if he added a frustrated sigh. "After what you've been through, I don't expect you to just trust me, but you can't stay here. It's not safe, with Gideon at large. I've got a Jeep parked on one of the ranch trails. It's not too far from here, only about a half mile, and Linnea and you could come with me. I could get you both back to town where you'll be safe."

Jace didn't dispute their safety once they were back in Culver Crossing. He could assign deputies for Linnea's protection detail and get himself to a hospital so a doctor could check his injuries. But leaving with Zimmerman could be many steps past a stupid move.

"Tell him to go get his Jeep," Linnea whispered. "Tell him you're injured and that you need him to bring it closer. Then, once he's gone, we'll leave, too. I don't see that we have a choice about staying here."

Neither did Jace. If Zimmerman was dirty, he'd try to kill them—either here in the cabin or once he had them in his vehicle. Of course, telling the agent that he was wounded might spur Zimmerman to charge the cabin without any further conversation. If that happened, then Jace would have to kill him.

"Gideon shot me," Jace called out to Zimmerman. He was going to take Linnea's plan and tweak it a little. "Go back to your Jeep and drive until you have phone reception. Then call the EMTs. They'll figure out a way to get to me."

Zimmerman stayed quiet several long moments. "How bad are you hurt?"

"Bad enough that I can't go walking through the woods. Not bad enough that I can't shoot straight. Go ahead," Jace insisted. "Leave now and get me some medical help. Then we can look for Gideon."

More hesitation from Zimmerman. "But what if Gideon comes after you while I'm gone?"

"I can shoot straight," Jace repeated. *Probably.* "Hurry. The sooner I'm out of here, the sooner I can help you find Gideon and Linnea."

But Zimmerman didn't hurry. "Linnea's really not with you?"

"No," Jace lied. "But we need to find her. Go now."

Zimmerman nodded, and he finally got moving. Jace had no idea how long it would take the agent to get to his vehicle. Or even if Zimmerman was truly headed in that direction. If he wasn't, then Zimmerman could be planning on circling around so he could sneak up on them and try to get into the cabin.

"We have to leave right now?" Linnea asked, but it didn't sound nearly as much like a question as it did a huge concern.

Which it was.

"Yeah. Zimmerman might go for backup. The wrong kind of backup," Jace emphasized.

She made a sound of agreement, hurried away from the window and pulled a rain poncho from the closet. Linnea put on a dull green hooded windbreaker and then draped the poncho around Jace. Since both items were still wet, he figured she'd used them when she'd rescued him.

"It's the best I can do," she said. "You can't put your shirt back on. Even if we could get it on, we'd risk opening up your wound."

Jace had already figured that out, and while the poncho was plenty bulky, it was still a challenge to get it on. A painful one. Hell. His shoulder felt as if someone was stabbing him with a knife. His head wasn't faring much better, and he hoped the pain didn't interfere with what he had to do.

He had to get Linnea to safety.

"This way," she instructed after she picked up the shotgun.

She led him out the front door. Not fast. Both of them paused in the doorway to look around. Thankfully, there were fewer trees in front of the cabin, which meant fewer places for someone to hide, but it was still possible for a person—mainly Gideon— to be lying in wait.

When they didn't see anyone, Linnea and he went into the yard. There were downed limbs from the storm, and the ground was a muddy bog. Still, they slogged their way through to the shed. Linnea used a remote that she took from her pocket to open it, and Jace saw that she'd been right about the size. It was plenty big enough to hold her car, the ATV and other equipment.

"I'll have to drive," she insisted.

Jace didn't argue with her. Couldn't. Besides, he wanted to keep his shooting hand free in case they ran into trouble.

The ATV had only one seat, which meant Linnea ended up in his lap. The pain was almost great enough for him not to notice the contact. Almost.

After she anchored the shotgun next to them, she started the engine and backed up. She didn't dawdle, but like him, let her gaze fire all around when she bolted away from the shed. That jostled Jace around and took care of the lust he was feeling for Linnea. The pain roared through him.

He blew out some sharp breaths, trying to steady himself, trying not to pass out. Losing consciousness sure as heck wouldn't do them any good.

The rain battered at them, but she maneuvered the ATV around the downed limbs and debris and kept on the road for about an eighth of a mile. Then Jace saw that the storm had indeed washed away enough of the dirt and gravel surface. There was now a huge ditch cutting through what had once been the road.

Slowing down, Linnea went around it, taking the ATV off the road and into an area thick with underbrush. Some of the bushes whipped at them as they passed, but she was finally able to cut around the ditch and get back on the road on the other side. It wasn't exactly smooth sailing after that, but she was able to pick up speed.

Even though his mobility was practically squat, Jace turned as much as possible so he could look behind them. No signs of Zimmerman or Gideon, and he prayed it would stay that way.

They hadn't gone far when Jace saw another spot where the road had washed out. Linnea went around it, and he tried to steel himself up for even more pain when the ATV bobbed over the uneven surface. Steeling didn't help much, but Linnea soon got them around it and headed toward the main road.

Almost immediately, though, she had to stop again and climb off the ATV to move a tree branch that was blocking their path.

That was Jace's cue to take out his phone, and relief washed through him when he saw that he finally had cell service. It was only one bar, but while he kept watch, he pressed the number for the sheriff's office. More relief came when one of his deputies, Glenn Spence, answered on the first ring.

"Jace, where the hell are you?" Glenn asked just as Linnea got back on his lap. Jace positioned the phone so that she could hear the conversation.

"Long story." Jace was about to request that his deputy send out an ambulance and backup, but Glenn continued before he could say anything else.

"Jace you need to get back here right now." Glenn's words ran together. "All hell is breaking loose."

Chapter Four

Even though Jace hadn't put the call on speaker, Linnea was practically head to head with him, and she had no trouble hearing what his deputy had just told him.

All hell is breaking loose.

Since that pretty much described the last twenty-four hours of her life, Linnea wasn't sure she could handle another dose of trouble. Especially since her own woes weren't over.

Jace and she weren't anywhere near safe yet, not with her brother and heaven knew how many of his lawbreaking cronies ready to gun them down. Plus, they had to worry about the ATF agent, Zimmerman. If he'd found the location of the cabin, then he knew about this road, and that meant he would at least consider the possibility they could use it to try to get away from him. Zimmerman might be able to come up on them from behind.

Jace groaned, probably a reaction to his pain and the news he'd just heard from his deputy. News that was no doubt important, but Linnea had her own priorities, and right now getting out of the woods with Jace was at the top of her list. That was why she didn't stop driving.

"Jace is hurt and needs help," she blurted out before Jace or Glenn could say anything else. She glanced around and tried to pinpoint their location. "We're on Smith Road, about two or three miles from the main highway. Get somebody out here ASAP. We're on an ATV and heading to the main road now."

She continued in that direction, trying to eat up some of the distance to get them out of the woods. She also kept watch, but sweet heaven, it was hard to see what she might need to see. Not only was the filmy curtain of rain stinging her eyes, but there were way too many thick trees, deep ditches and shrubs that tangled and blended with the landscape. A sniper would have his pick of places to hide and lie in wait.

"Boss?" she heard Glenn say. "You're really hurt?"

"I am," Jace confirmed. "I'll fill you in when I get to the office. What's going on there?"

"Hold a second and let me call dispatch so I can get you some help," Glenn insisted.

Linnea drove on. Because of all the debris and washed-away parts of the road, she was going practically at a snail's pace, which, of course, was making them an easy target.

"All right." Glenn's voice came back on several long moments later. "Crystal and some EMTs are headed your way. They'll turn on Smith Road and just keep going until they find you."

Crystal was Deputy Crystal Rankin, and Linnea would be thankful to have that kind of backup. Despite Jace's assurances that he could fire a gun even with his injuries, Linnea just wasn't buying it. Since her own aim was in question, as well, they needed all the help they could get.

"Tell me what's wrong there at the sheriff's office," Jace asked.

Glenn certainly didn't jump in with an explanation. Odd, considering how anxious he had been when he first answered Jace's call.

"Uh, is that Linnea with you?" Glenn asked.

Linnea was surprised the deputy had recognized her voice. She'd met Glenn, of course, but since he'd moved to Culver Crossing only a couple of years earlier, she didn't know him well and had only spoken to him a few times. So, why would Glenn have assumed she was the one with Jace?

Jace hesitated, too. Long enough for Glenn to continue.

"Was it Linnea who hurt you?" the deputy pressed, and every word of that question dripped with concern.

She hissed out a breath. Linnea hadn't understood the concern in Glenn's voice, but she sure as heck got it now.

"No," Jace snarled. "Why the hell would you ask that?"

Linnea wanted to know the same thing, and she figured whatever Glenn's answer was, it wouldn't be good.

"Because, well, because Toby Conway's body was found at his house," Glenn said. "He was murdered, boss. Not an easy death, either. A gut shot and two more shots to his kneecaps."

That felt like a punch to her own gut. Not because Linnea cared about or even liked Toby, but because she was very much afraid that Gideon had done this.

And that made her brother a killer.

She bit back a sob and tears. Neither would help now, and she continued to maneuver the ATV, inching them closer and closer to the EMTs and backup.

"There's more," Glenn continued a moment later. "Right before he died, Toby scrawled out a message that we found next to his body. He said it was Linnea who shot him and left him to die."

Linnea automatically hit the brakes, and this time the gut punch was a lot worse. "What?" she managed to say into the phone.

"He claimed you killed him," Glenn spelled out.

Linnea tried to mentally latch on to that. Tried to make sense of it. She couldn't. But apparently Jace didn't have any trouble working through his thoughts, because he sounded like a cop when he snapped out the next question to Glenn.

"When did Toby die?" Jace demanded.

"The ME just got the body, so we don't have a time of death yet," Glenn answered without a moment's hesitation this time. "But it appears to have been late last night or very early this morning."

Either time meant she didn't have an alibi. Well, she did. She'd been taking Jace to the cabin and trying to keep him alive during that time frame, but Jace wouldn't be able to verify that since he'd been unconscious.

"I didn't kill Toby," Linnea insisted. "I didn't."

"We'll get it straightened out," Jace assured her. "My guess is Gideon killed Toby and tried to set up Linnea."

Since Glenn didn't question why Gideon would have done that, it meant the deputy at least knew about her brother being a fugitive. Of course, he did. Everyone would know that the ATF was on his trail. Maybe Glenn would then follow this through and at least consider that a dirty cop would continue being dirty and eliminate Toby, the man who'd ratted him out to Jace.

"We found a knife and an earring at the scene of Toby's murder," Glenn went on. "I sent them to the lab to be analyzed."

They wouldn't be hers. But Linnea immediately rethought that. Maybe they were. Maybe they'd been taken from her house. It wouldn't have been hard for Gideon to get in since he had a key and knew the code for her security system.

"I've never even been to Toby's," she muttered, but Linnea didn't add more. Jace was right that they could work out all of this later. It wasn't the time for her to try to prove her innocence while she still needed to get Jace to those EMTs.

"Toby said in the note he left that Linnea is the one who sold the weapons and drugs," Glenn explained. "That she used Gideon's ID and badge to get the stash from the SAPD storage."

That was so outrageous a claim that it dried up any hint of tears or sobs. Yes, Gideon had done this all right, and he was going to try to pin the blame on her. Fury raged through her, followed by the sickening dread that her brother was the monster she was beginning to fear he was.

"You'll have Toby's note analyzed, to make sure he actually wrote it?" she asked. When Glenn made a sound of agreement, Linnea added, "Even if it is his handwriting, that doesn't mean he wrote it voluntarily. He probably would have written any and everything if someone had a gun to his head."

Again, that got a sound of agreement from Glenn.

Just in case Jace had any doubts whatsoever about her innocence, she glanced back at him to repeat that she hadn't done any of the things Toby had claimed in his note, when she saw him lift the edge of the poncho and look at his shoulder.

Blood.

The wound had obviously reopened, and blood was seeping out of the bandage and onto his forearm. Added to that, Jace was shivering now. That could be just because of the rain, but it was also possible he was going into shock. It was one of the things the medical book had said could happen.

"Tell the EMTs to hurry," Linnea ordered Glenn. "Jace is hurt bad." And she got the ATV moving as fast as she could. Every minute counted now.

"I will," Glenn assured them just as Jace ended the call.

With plenty of effort Jace put his phone in between his stomach and her back, probably to keep the rain off it, and then she felt him shifting his gun, which must've strained him even more.

"How far to the main road?" he asked, his breathing labored now.

"Not far," she lied.

At the pace they were going, it could be another twenty minutes or so before they got there, but hopefully that time would be shortened considerably since the EMTs were heading their way.

"Lean your head on my shoulder," she instructed. "You're not looking your best, Hotshot."

"Hotshot," he repeated in a mumble.

She kept her attention on the road, but Linnea

thought maybe Jace attempted to chuckle. He remembered that was what she'd called him when she was a teenager. The nickname she'd given him because he'd been so darn good at pretty much everything. Working with the cutting horses, bull riding, football—you name it, Jace had excelled at it.

That included snagging her attention and never letting go.

Linnea suspected that part of Jace's drive to be the best stemmed from his miserable childhood. There'd been a whopping big scandal when his father's affair with a wealthy married woman had led to the woman's husband committing suicide. That, in turn, had caused Jace's parents to split, with neither one of them taking much interest in him after that. It was one of the reasons he'd spent so much time hanging out with Gideon.

"I'm not feeling like a hotshot right now," he added.

Linnea made a sound of agreement and thought Jace's voice seemed weaker. She reconsidered that, though, when she felt him move. With surprising speed, he shifted his position, bringing up his gun.

That gave her a jolt of adrenaline, but before she could even say anything, Jace hooked his uninjured arm around her waist.

"Get down," he snapped.

He didn't wait for her to do that, though. Jace pulled her off the seat and onto the muddy road.

It was just in the nick of time. Because a bullet slammed into the front end of the ATV.

Linnea hadn't needed anything to get her heart pounding and her blood racing, but that did it. The fear quickly replaced her shock and confusion, and she knew exactly why Jace had done what he had.

They were under attack.

She hadn't even seen the gunman, but she could certainly hear him. A third shot ricocheted off the ATV, the sound of metal bouncing off metal and pinging through the woods.

Jace got them moving again, though she could hear his grunts and groans of pain. He rolled them right into a water-filled ditch that was about three feet deep. Not ideal, but it was a lot better than being on the ATV, where they could have been shot.

Of course, they could still be shot.

Hindsight sucked, because only minutes earlier, Linnea had been thinking how easy it would have been for a sniper to hide. And she'd been right. She hadn't even seen anyone. But Jace obviously had, and thankfully, he'd reacted in time to save them. Although the save had probably come with a Texas-sized price tag attached to it.

Jace's groans were louder now, and he arched against the pain, causing his phone to drop into the water before Linnea could latch onto it. However, she did manage to grab his gun.

Another shot came their way. It didn't hit the

ATV this time but instead smacked into the ditch and sent mud and gravel flying right at them. She couldn't be sure, but she thought the gunman had shifted his position.

Moving closer to them.

Or rather moving in for the kill.

"Stay down," Jace warned her when she started to lever up.

Linnea hadn't even thought about staying down, not with a possible killer closing in on them. But she forced herself to stay put and listen. She didn't hear any footsteps. Only the rain and their heavy gusting breaths.

"Is it Gideon firing those shots?" she whispered.

"Don't know. I didn't get a good look at him."

So it could be a lackey. Or Zimmerman. Heck, it could be a hunter with poor eyesight who'd mistaken them for deer. But Linnea knew that was just wishful thinking on her part. After what had happened to Jace, it was obvious this was yet another attempt to do away with the lawman who'd tried to arrest her brother.

Since the shooter obviously knew their exact location, Linnea decided to try something. Probably something stupid. But maybe there was a vein of brotherly love left in Gideon.

"Gideon?" she called out, and she held her breath, waiting for him to respond. Praying that the sound of her voice would bring him back to his senses.

No answer. Well, not a verbal one anyway. But there was another blast of gunfire, and this one came even closer to Jace and her. So much for coming back to his senses. Instead, it seemed to serve as a reminder that he wanted them dead.

"Hand me my gun," Jace said, and despite the fact that he had no color left in his face, took it from her.

"I have a better chance of shooting him than you do," Linnea insisted.

But she might as well have been talking to the rain, because Jace climbed over her, putting himself in front of her like a shield. Later, she'd give him some grief over trying to protect her this way, but giving grief could get them both killed. Right now, she gave Jace the quiet he needed to focus.

And focusing was obviously what he was doing.

He didn't make a sound, but he lifted his head a fraction. Listening. Linnea tried to do that, as well, but she certainly didn't hear a gunman coming their way. However, Jace must have, because he levered himself up, and in the same motion, took aim at something.

And he fired.

The sound roared through her ears and head, and Linnea thought she might have cried out. Hard to tell, though, because the gun blast was the only thing she could hear. It echoed and expanded, filling her with throbbing pain.

Apparently, Jace didn't seem to have that problem. He shifted a couple of inches. Aimed. Fired again. And again.

Linnea tried to push aside the pain and figure out if he'd hit his intended target. She couldn't tell. But she did hear something else. Something she definitely wanted to hear.

A siren.

It was the wail of an approaching ambulance, and she thought maybe there was a cop's siren in the mix, as well. Relief surged, but Jace clearly wasn't on the same page with her. She heard him curse, and he practically climbed over her to get out of the ditch.

"The SOB's getting away," Jace spat out.

Linnea didn't want that. She wanted the snake caught. Even if the snake turned out to be her brother. But Jace certainly wasn't in any shape to go in pursuit.

That didn't stop him from trying, though.

Jace made it out of the ditch and even got a yard or so before she saw him drop down onto his knees. Mercy, he was going to kill himself by bleeding out if she didn't stop him.

She first tried to latch onto the side of the ditch so she could get out, but her hands just slid through the mud. Cursing, she grabbed some tree roots that were poking through the side of the ditch, and used them like a rope to start climbing.

Despite his injuries, Jace had made it look easy.

It wasn't. Her boots bogged into the mud, and her hands were slick, so she lost her grip a couple of times. It seemed to take hours for her to finally make it to the top. She hit solid ground and started moving. Fast. The moment she reached Jace, she took hold of him and pulled him into her arms.

Linnea heard it then.

Over the wail of the sirens, the rain and Jace's ragged breath, she cursed the running footsteps of their attacker getting away.

Chapter Five

Pain. That was the one sensation that came through loud and clear for Jace. Unfortunately, his mind wasn't nearly so clear, and it took him a moment to push through the agony and realize that he wasn't back in the cabin. Or in the ditch with a gunman shooting at Linnea and him.

He was in the hospital.

Before he even opened his eyes, he could smell the antiseptic in the air and hear the pulsing beeps of a machine. A machine he realized was monitoring him.

"Hell," he grumbled.

He hadn't wanted to be brought to the hospital. He'd spelled that out to the EMTs when they'd arrived. They were to treat him so he could get back to work. Of course, everything was fuzzy after he'd given that order, and he was positive that he'd lost consciousness. Hard to argue with EMTs when you were out like a light.

Speaking of lights, the ones overhead caused him

to wince in more pain. Jace gathered his breath, steeled himself and blinked until his eyes could adjust to the brightness. Even then, there was pain, but it was a drop in the bucket compared to his shoulder. Only then did he remember threatening the EMTs so they wouldn't give him any pain meds.

Obviously, that hadn't been a smart thing for him to do.

Wincing, he lifted his head and looked around, hoping he was safe here. Glenn would have seen to that, Jace assured himself. But his deputy wasn't around. No medical personnel, either. However, Linnea was in a chair, staring at him from over the rim of a to-go container of what smelled like the flowery tea that he knew she liked to drink. She was wearing green scrubs, and she set aside a newspaper that she'd had on her lap.

"What's a four-letter word for somebody who does something stupid?" Linnea asked, getting to her feet and putting her hand on his chest to stop him when he tried to get up.

He frowned. "I'm not up to helping with a crossword right now."

"The answer is *Jace. J-a-c-e*," she spelled out.

His frown deepened. Jace had figured she would dole out some TLC or at least ask how he was feeling, but Linnea definitely had no such ideas. She seemed riled.

"You tore open your gunshot wound when you

jumped out of that ditch," she continued. "You left cover to charge at a guy who was shooting at you even though you were in no shape to shoot back."

Oh, that. He certainly hadn't forgotten about it, but what he'd done had been pure instinct and training.

"I'm a cop," Jace reminded her. "I didn't want the idiot getting away." He paused, muttered some choice curse words when he remembered how all of that had played out. "The shooter got away, didn't he? Was Crystal or one of my other deputies able to find him?"

"He got away," Linnea confirmed. "Because Crystal and the EMTs were more concerned about putting you in the ambulance and getting you here to the hospital so the doctors could save your life."

Linnea stared at him with slightly narrowed eyes. Then she sighed. Softened. There was no other word for her. The tightness in her face went slack, her mouth trembled and concern pushed aside the anger in her eyes.

Concern for him.

Yeah, Jace got that, too. He hadn't been close to dying, at least he didn't think he had been, but Linnea had saved him. Not just by taking him to the cabin but also putting him on that ATV and driving him out of those woods. If they'd stayed at the cabin, the gunman could have pinned them down and sent a hail of bullets through the flimsy wood walls.

Because Linnea had saved him and because he knew he'd scared her spitless when he jumped out of that ditch, he reached out, took her hand and gave it a gentle squeeze. Even that small movement hurt, and she noticed, too. She reached for the intercom button on his bed.

"Wait," Jace said. He wanted to talk to a nurse or doctor, but he needed to get some info from Linnea first. "Is this room secured? Are you safe?"

She nodded. "The hospital security guard is right outside your door."

That was a start, but the Culver Crossing Hospital wasn't large enough to have a full team of security guards. If the gunman who'd tried to kill them wanted to get into his room, all he'd have to do was create some kind of distraction to pull the security guard away from the door. Jace might not be able to protect Linnea if that happened. Especially since his gun was nowhere in sight.

"I need to talk to Glenn," he said.

"Glenn just left about twenty minutes ago," Linnea informed him. "He's making arrangements to send over a reserve deputy who'll stay until you're discharged."

Which would happen soon. Jace would insist on that. "I need my gun. Where is it?"

The softness on her face wavered some, and while Linnea didn't exactly roll her eyes, she looked as if that was exactly what she wanted to do. "Glenn took it with him. You weren't allowed to be armed when you were unconscious. Hospital rules. It's a security risk."

"Well, I'm conscious now, and I want my gun back," he snarled. He reached for his phone, which was always in his pocket.

It wasn't there, of course, and he remembered that he'd dropped it in the bloody ditch. He also didn't have a pocket. Or jeans. Or boxers, for that matter. He was naked except for a green gown that he was certain would show his bare butt when he stood.

"Our clothes were wet," Linnea explained as if she knew exactly what he was thinking. "You had to be stripped down again, and your gunshot wound had to be cleaned and stitched."

Jace had some vague memories of all of that. More memories of pain, too. And of some kind of medication being put in his IV. An IV that was still in the back of his hand.

"Someone drugged me," he recalled.

"*Someone*—" she repeated, mocking his tone, "—aka Dr. Garcia—gave you meds so he could tend your wound without you passing out or yelling from the pain. He then dosed you with plenty of antibiotics so you wouldn't get an infection."

"I wouldn't have yelled," Jace growled, and to prove it, he sat up. Oh, man. The pain was indeed bad, but he stayed upright on sheer willpower. "How long have I been here anyway?"

"A little while." She huffed and said, "About five hours," when he continued to stare at her.

"Five hours with a killer at large and our lives at risk." He definitely wouldn't be thanking Dr. Garcia for dosing him up. "I need to call Glenn and get an update on the investigation."

A murder investigation at that. Jace had only gotten the broad strokes when it came to Toby, but there should be plenty of details by now.

"Glenn will be back soon, and he'll fill you in," Linnea assured him. "And bring you your weapon." She gently took hold of his good shoulder and eased him back down. "But as for updates, I've already told you the gunman's still at large. Gideon, too," she added. "Of course, Gideon could have been the gunman."

That was true, and Jace would have given up his paycheck to have gotten a glimpse of the shooter's face. If it wasn't Gideon, then it was likely his partner in crime. Or maybe a hired hitman. But still, Jace wished he knew what he was up against. The more hired guns, the greater the threat.

"Glenn ran a background check on Zimmerman," she added. "He didn't find any obvious signs that he was dirty."

"I want Glenn to keep looking," Jace snarled.

"So do I, and he will." She paused. "I didn't kill Toby," Linnea stated while she continued to stare down at him. She seemed to be looking for any signs that he doubted her.

He didn't.

"I know," Jace assured her. "His death is on Gideon or whoever he's partnered with."

"Maybe another cop," she provided. "Or somebody else in law enforcement like Zimmerman."

Yeah, it was the *somebody else* that was eating away at him. Jace knew the threat Gideon could pose, but now he'd have to look at others he didn't know.

Jace kept the eye contact with her because this was something Linnea needed to hear. "When I was chasing Gideon, he never once tried to convince me that he was innocent. Just the opposite. He seemed fine with dirtying his badge and putting guns in the hands of criminals who could use them for heaven knows what. He wants us both dead. Best for us to get past that and focus on stopping him."

He hadn't exactly sugarcoated that last bit, the bit she truly needed to take to heart. Jace didn't pretty up the next part, either.

"If it comes to a showdown between Gideon and me," he added, "I'll have to kill him."

She nodded, swallowed hard. "I know. If it comes down to us or him, I expect you to kill him."

Her voice broke. The tears came. Tears that she cursed and tried to blink back and bat away by fanning her hand in front of her face. Jace couldn't fault her for those tears. He was torn up about this, too.

"I didn't see this in Gideon," Jace said. "Didn't know he was capable of doing something like this." There was an implied *Did you?* at the end of that.

Linnea shook her head. "When I found out, I didn't want it to be true."

Their gazes held, and she swiped away a tear that she hadn't managed to stave off, just as the door opened. Jace automatically braced himself for a fight, and he took hold of Linnea's arm, instinctively wanting to move her behind him. Of course, he couldn't manage that since he was in bed, but he soon realized that it wasn't necessary.

Dr. Ed Garcia came in.

He'd known the doctor most of his life—everyone in Culver Crossing did—and Dr. Garcia had stitched him up a couple of times before this. He trusted the doctor despite the dose of pain meds he'd administered.

Dr. Garcia gave Jace a long once-over, made a sound that could have meant anything, before he glanced at Linnea. "I need to examine Jace," he told her. "You can wait with Hal, the security guard, if you want."

"No, she can't," Jace insisted before she could say anything. "Linnea's in my protective custody."

The doctor lifted an eyebrow and motioned toward the huge bandage peeking out from the top of the gown. "Are you in any shape for protective custody work?" he asked, some dryness in his tone.

"I'll protect her," Jace said as a way of avoiding the question. He wasn't sure he wanted to know the answer to that, but Jace figured if it came down to another gunfight, he'd do what was necessary.

Even if it hurt like hell.

He had an easier time interpreting the next sound the doctor made. It was a definite *suit yourself*, with a layer of skepticism tossed in.

"FYI," the doctor continued as he lowered the front of Jace's hospital gown and lifted the bandage to take a look at the wound. "Linnea did a decent job of fixing you up."

Jace knew that, and he gave Linnea a nod of thanks. He might not have died if she hadn't found him, but if Gideon or one of his cronies had gotten to him first, his chances of survival wouldn't have been good.

"You're lucky," Dr. Garcia went on. "The bullet cut through some muscle but not the bone. It's a clean through-and-through. Now that you're stitched up, I suspect you'll heal fast enough. At least you will if you take it easy for a couple of days and wear a sling so that your arm doesn't move around a lot."

That was mostly good news, especially the part about him healing fast. But the taking it easy wouldn't happen. Nor was it necessary. He'd been shot in his left shoulder, and he didn't need that part of his body to fire a shot to defend himself and Linnea.

"Your pain meds have worn off." The doctor pressed the bandage back in place. "I can have a nurse bring you another dose."

"No." And Jace couldn't say that fast enough. "I need a clear head, not one clouded by drugs."

"Your head won't be so clear if you're hurting," the doctor mumbled, adding another grunt that seemed to say, "Suit yourself."

Jace would indeed suit himself, and that started with him getting out of here. "I have to get back to work, so I need you to discharge me."

"The earliest I can release you is tomorrow." The doctor huffed when Jace opened his mouth to object to that. "You were shot and lost a lot of blood. Like I said, Linnea did a good job patching you up, but we have to take precautions. One day," he emphasized, his gaze drifting to Linnea. "And I'll arrange it so she can stay with you if she wants."

"It's what I want," Linnea rushed to say.

Jace seriously doubted that was because she had a yen to sleep in a chair by his hospital bed. Nope. Her wish to stay might not even be tied to her protective custody. Knowing Linnea, she probably wanted to be there to help him fight off Gideon if he showed up. That had Jace reconsidering if he should have her go with one of his deputies.

"If you're staying, I'm staying," Linnea insisted, staring at Jace.

So, either she'd developed ESP, or for a second time today, she'd rightly interpreted his thoughts.

"He's staying," the doctor insisted right along with her. "Make sure he doesn't overdo it."

"I will," she assured Dr. Garcia, though Jace knew there was no way she could back that up.

"I need to get out of here," Jace insisted, but the doctor didn't respond. Not verbally anyway. Dr. Garcia wrote something on a chart that he slipped into a slot on the door, and left.

Jace immediately shifted his attention to Linnea, and cursed. The profanity wasn't aimed at her, though, but rather the doctor, who'd clearly not listened to him.

Using his right hand, Jace threw back the cover, sat up and swung his legs to the side of the bed. Oh, yeah. The movement hurt, but it was something he was sure he could work through.

Well, he was almost sure.

"I need my gun, a phone and a laptop." He snapped out the words. "The sooner I get started on this investigation, the better. In fact, I need crime scene photos of Toby's murder. And if Glenn hasn't done it already, I want a crime scene team out to the area where Gideon and I traded bullets."

Staring at him, Linnea walked closer, and closer, until she was standing between his legs. It was a darn effective way of stopping him from getting off the bed, since he'd have a hard time moving her.

"Remember that time you kissed me?" she asked, mentally throwing him off balance.

Jace had expected a lecture as to why he couldn't get or do all those things he'd just grumbled about. Or an attempt to placate him by saying she'd see what she could do about the two easiest items on his list—a phone and a laptop. But nowhere in the possibilities of her responses had he considered that she'd bring up that kiss.

"I was eighteen," she continued when he gaped at her. "You took my hand, laced our fingers together and leaned in. Only lips to lips. That and our hands were the only physical contact, but you made it count." She smiled almost wistfully, as if savoring the memory.

Jace was savoring it, as well. A little too much. She'd tasted both hot and sweet. Oh, and forbidden. Definitely that.

He tried to shift the conversation and therefore the memory avalanche. "You're trying to distract me, to stop me from being so pissed off."

No wistful smile this time. It took on a sly edge. "Did it work?"

It had. And that wasn't a good thing. No way did he need to be thinking about that kiss or kissing her again.

But he was.

That made him feel both sick and brainless. Her life was at risk, and he didn't need the distraction of this, well, heat between them. It had always been there, but it had kicked up several serious notches. Maybe because of the shared danger. Nearly dying together had a way of bulldozing through any barriers, including those that should have stayed in place.

Again, he went for a conversation shift and a complete realignment of his thoughts. "I need to get out of here," he repeated.

"You need to heal," she reminded him right back. "How are you going to protect me if you're too hurt to stop the bad guys?"

Well, at least she hadn't said, *How are you going to kiss me if you're too hurt?* That meant she had more common sense than he did right now. Still, Jace focused on the things he needed—and no, kissing Linnea wasn't anywhere on that list. He was about to ask for her help in getting a phone and a laptop, when there was a knock at the door.

Again, Jace moved, and this time he actually made it off the bed and to his feet. He wasn't a hundred percent, maybe not even fifty percent, but he didn't fall on his butt. Nor was there a threat. Because it was Glenn who poked his head in and smiled when he saw Jace standing.

"Didn't expect you to be out of bed," the deputy commented, stepping inside.

"He's not supposed to be." Linnea moved in

again, taking hold of Jace's hips and pushing until he sat down.

Jace frowned and nudged her away so he could talk to Glenn. Or rather give Glenn some orders. "I want my gun, a phone and laptop."

"Sure, boss. Figured you would." Glenn set a backpack on the small table next to Jace's bed. "I added a change of clothes that I got from your locker. A charger cord, too, for the phone."

"Thanks," Jace mumbled, reaching for the backpack. Then, shifting and reaching again with his good arm. "I wish Dr. Garcia was as efficient as you are."

Glenn put his hands on his hips. "Guess that means he's not springing you loose, huh?"

"Not today." Jace didn't waste much time on the scowl he aimed at Glenn. Instead, he got busy taking out the items from the backpack. "But that doesn't mean I can't get some work done. I want any reports you have on Toby's murder."

The deputy nodded but suddenly looked very uneasy, and that discomfort was definitely aimed at Linnea.

"It's all right," Jace assured him. "Linnea didn't kill Toby, so it's okay if she hears what you have to say." Besides, Jace was holding to his rule about not letting Linnea out of his sight.

"Okay," Glenn said, gathering his breath. "Along with being shot three times, Toby was also stabbed in the chest, and the knife was left at the scene. The knife appears to have been taken from a knife block in Linnea's kitchen."

Linnea groaned. "I guess Gideon or whoever did this wanted to make sure the cops looked at me for this. But along with the note that Toby left, it's too obvious."

She seemed surprised and relieved that both Glenn and Jace nodded in agreement. Linnea studied their expressions and shook her head.

"So, why would Gideon have done that?" she asked. "First of all, my house is less than a block off Main Street, where he could have been spotted."

"Maybe Gideon had someone else break in," Jace suggested. "Or if he wasn't hurt that bad, he could have sneaked into the place last night. You don't have neighbors behind you, so he could have gone through your backyard."

"Yes," she muttered but then shook her head again. "Gideon's a cop, and he'd know the scene would look like an obvious plant. A blatant attempt to make me look guilty. Why wouldn't he throttle back on that?"

Jace had already turned this over in his mind when he first spoke to Glenn on the phone about it. "I figure Gideon knows we'll be looking at him no matter what so-called evidence is left or found at the scene. He's the one with a strong motive to kill Toby. Not you."

"Well, according to that so-called evidence, I stole the guns and drugs," she reminded him.

"And that's just dirt to muddy the waters," Jace answered. "There's absolutely no evidence that you used his badge to go into warehouses and steal confiscated items. No evidence that you'd know how to fence such things even if they came into your possession. Right, Glenn?"

"Right," the deputy verified. "I'm sorry, Linnea." He scrubbed his hand over his face. "I know it must hurt for you to hear all the things your brother's done."

"It does hurt," she said under her breath. "It hurts even more to know that he wants Jace and me dead. Gideon's basically thrown away the first three decades of his life as if they didn't matter." She paused again. "Why?"

"Money," Jace and Glenn answered together. "Lots of money," Jace emphasized.

And with that reminder, he thought it'd be easier for Linnea to suss out her brother's motive. Gideon had always loved the finer things, but his family had been ranchers and hadn't always had a lot of ready cash to give him those things. Jace, and probably Linnea, as well, had overlooked Gideon's thirst for more, more, more, but that thirst had likely been the reason for what was going on now. Added to that, Gideon was cocky enough to believe that he'd never get caught.

Silence settled over the room for several long moments before Glenn cleared his throat, obviously pulling himself back from his thoughts about Gideon.

"I've set up a schedule so your door will be guarded by the reserve deputies," Glenn explained. "The Mercy Ridge Sheriff's office called and offered to help us with that if needed."

That was a surprise since the sheriff of the neighboring town of Mercy Ridge was Barrett Logan, and Jace and he weren't exactly pals. Of course, that non-pal status wasn't based on anything recent that had happened. Years ago, Jace's dad had had an affair with Barrett's mom. An affair that had ended disastrously and created a couple of decades of bad blood between the families. But obviously, Barrett didn't let bad blood get in the way of offering help to a fellow officer.

"I'll call Barrett and thank him," Jace said. Heck, he'd even take Barrett up on his offer if it meant keeping Linnea safe.

"Anything else you need me to do?" Glenn asked a moment later. "Anything else you need at all?" He extended that question to Linnea.

She shook her head. "A nurse gave me a toiletry kit and another pair of scrubs. That'll be enough for tonight. Maybe tomorrow, I can go to my house and get some things."

Jace didn't offer her any hope on that. "Even if

the CSIs are done, it's not safe for you to go back there. Gideon could be watching the place."

Though that last part was a stretch. There was enough gossip in Culver Crossing for Gideon to have heard exactly where Jace and Linnea were. It would be gutsy to come after them at the hospital, but Gideon had already proven the gutsy side of himself by trying to gun down Jace.

"All right, then I'll head out," Glenn said as he tipped his head to the backpack he'd brought in. "All the reports on Toby are in your email, and I'll make sure you get any updates. Call me when you're sprung tomorrow to let me know where you'll be going."

Jace started to say that he'd be heading to his office. Which he would do. But it wasn't a place where Linnea could stay long-term, and that meant Jace had to give it some thought.

"I'll call you," Jace assured him.

Glenn turned, opened the door and practically ran into the wide-shouldered man who'd been about to knock. Jace instantly recognized him. Lieutenant Bryce Cannon, Gideon's boss at San Antonio PD.

"He said he's a cop," the security guard relayed. "And I had him show me his badge. I wouldn't have let him in without asking you first, though."

Jace slid his hand over his gun, which was still in the backpack. He didn't know Bryce that well, had only met him a time or two at cookouts and such at Gideon's. Jace had heard nothing about him to make him believe he was dirty. Still, best not to take chances, because Gideon had had help on the criminal path he'd taken, and he could have gotten that from his boss.

"Sorry to bother you," Bryce said, stepping inside the room.

Linnea knew Bryce, as well, and had probably socialized with him a lot more than Jace had. In fact, Jace had heard Gideon mention something about Bryce and Linnea dating. But that had been a while back. Years ago. So, obviously, things hadn't worked out between them.

She moved closer to Jace, putting her body right next to his. Glenn must have picked up on the suddenly tense vibe, because he stayed put.

"Did you find Gideon?" Jace asked the lieutenant.

"No. Not yet, but I've got plenty of men out looking for him."

Men who could be in league with Gideon. This was definitely not the time to trust anyone who'd worked with him.

"But that's not why I'm here," Bryce continued. His attention wasn't on Jace but on Linnea. "There's a problem, and I wanted to let you know what was heading your way."

Because the back of her hand was touching his, Jace felt her go stiff. "What problem?" she asked.

Bryce took a moment before he responded. "There's an ATF agent, Lionel Zimmerman."

"I met him," Linnea said when Bryce didn't add more. "Is he dead?"

Bryce blinked, clearly surprised by her question. "No. He's very much alive. Or at least he was a half hour ago when he called me. He wanted to give me a heads-up that he'd be coming to Culver Crossing this afternoon."

"Why?" she pressed.

"I'm sorry, Linnea." Bryce lowered his head, shook it. "But Zimmerman's coming here to arrest you."

Chapter Six

Linnea figured she should be shocked or furious with what Bryce had just told her, but she could thank the bone-weary fatigue from spent adrenaline for keeping her response low-key.

Unlike Jace.

He cursed, belting out some very bad words along with shooting eye daggers at Bryce. "Zimmerman can go to hell. He's not arresting Linnea." Jace growled out more profanity. "She didn't kill Toby. She was framed."

Bryce dragged in a weary-sounding breath. Weary because he might have thought of himself as just the messenger of this bad news. "Zimmerman wants to arrest Linnea for what he believes is her part in the transfer and sale of the guns and drugs that Gideon stole," he reminded Jace.

It wasn't the first time today that she'd been accused of that. It was in the "dying" note that Toby had left. A note that had yet to be verified as the real deal. Linnea suspected that Gideon had planted other "evidence" just in case the cops and feds needed more ammunition to look in her direction.

"I'm sorry," Bryce told her, and his tone practically screamed of the old intimacy between them. And there had been some intimacy.

Sort of.

She'd dated Bryce for about a month, and before that, they'd hung out whenever they were at Gideon's at the same time. They'd never had sex, though. She just hadn't been that into him, but Bryce had apparently been into her.

When she ended things, he hadn't exactly turned stalker, but he'd called her multiple times to ask her to reconsider. Had sent her flowers. And had even talked Gideon into trying to sway her into giving him another chance.

It hadn't worked.

And when Bryce hadn't gotten her to cave, he'd turned petty by insulting her to mutual friends. He'd also given her the cold shoulder and even some nasty glances when they ended up at the same social functions. That was why things were awkward between them, and that *intimate* tone only made it more so.

Linnea hoped that Bryce wouldn't use this mess of a situation to try to rekindle things between them or to vent more of his venom about her. But she pushed that possibility aside. For now. She pushed everything aside except for this latest development.

"Zimmerman must think he has proof of my wrongdoing if he plans to arrest me," Linnea pointed out.

"He's not arresting you," Jace snapped.

"I agree," Bryce said, giving a nod to Linnea to let her know he was addressing her comment, "but that's Zimmerman's plan. He says he got eyewitness statements from an anonymous source that detail your involvement."

That didn't improve Jace's mood. "His anonymous source is Gideon," he snarled. "Or maybe Zimmerman himself. Because any idiot who'd plan to arrest Linnea on evidence like that is suspect at best."

"I agree," Bryce repeated, and his quietly spoken agreement finally had Jace simmering down. "I'm not even sure Zimmerman managed to get a warrant for an arrest. I doubt he did. He's riled though because in his mind, you sneaked out of the cabin after he offered you help."

"Help I couldn't trust," Jace pointed out.

"I know," the lieutenant agreed. "But I suspect he plans to come here, throw his federal weight around and try to take Linnea into custody for questioning. I know you won't let that happen," he quickly added before Jace could object.

Maybe it was all that awkwardness playing into this, but Linnea didn't think Bryce was paying Jace a compliment. It seemed to be more of an…observation. One with undertones that she could spin back to their breakup. Crud. Did Bryce think Jace and she were together? If so, she didn't want any jealousy, even tiny bits of it, playing into this.

Bryce shifted his attention back to her. "You shouldn't be arrested," he stated. "Because Zimmerman might be as dirty as Gideon."

Since Jace and she had already come to that conclusion, that wasn't exactly a news flash, but she was hoping that Bryce had something to back up that accusation. Of course, she'd also considered that Bryce might be her brother's partner in crime. If that was true, then he was even more dangerous than Gideon. After all, there wasn't a statewide search going on for Bryce. He could use his badge to come and go as he pleased.

Including into Jace's hospital room.

Thank heaven Glenn had put Jace's gun in the backpack. But maybe it wouldn't be necessary for them to use it.

"Please tell me you have any shred of proof that Zimmerman and Gideon have teamed up," Jace said.

Bryce shook his head. "But I do have a lead." Again, he looked at Linnea. "Tammy Wheatly is missing, and I think she's on the run with Gideon."

"Tammy," she repeated on a groan, and she looked at Jace to fill him in.

"I know who she is," Jace said before she could

explain. "She's Gideon's criminal informant turned girlfriend."

Linnea pulled back her shoulders. She'd known about the CI part but not the other. "Gideon and Tammy are involved?"

"Yeah," Jace answered as Bryce made a sound of agreement.

It was Bryce who continued. "Though *involved* maybe isn't the right word for it. I think it was just sex for Gideon." He stopped, his forehead bunching up. "It could be a whole lot more for Tammy. Gideon mentioned that she was getting clingy."

"Clingy?" Linnea repeated on a huff.

This was the first she was hearing about any of this, but it shouldn't have surprised her. Gideon didn't make a habit of discussing his sex partners with her. Especially a sex partner who shouldn't be one.

"Did either one of you tell Gideon that it wasn't a smart idea for a cop to sleep around with a CI?" Linnea threw out there. "I mean, the *C* in CI stands for *criminal*."

"I counseled him about it," Bryce answered. "He agreed to end things with her. That was two days ago."

That was the day before her brother had tried to kill Jace. So maybe there hadn't been time for a breakup. It was also possible that Gideon had never intended to end the relationship with Tammy.

She studied Bryce's expression. "You think Tammy helped him with his illegal guns and drug operation. You believe she could still be helping him."

"I do," Bryce said without hesitation. "Tammy's finished her parole for drug possession, but according to some of the other CIs, she's kept up with her old contacts. She'd be able to get the drugs to buyers. Maybe the guns, too. That's why I wanted to talk to her, but when I went to her place in San Antonio, her landlord and neighbors said they haven't seen her in days."

That didn't necessarily mean that Tammy was with Gideon, but it was possible. It was also possible that the woman was just off with friends. Still, it was suspicious.

"I'm getting a warrant to have some detectives go into Tammy's place," Bryce continued a moment later. "If she's really involved in this, she might not have left anything incriminating behind, but maybe we'll get lucky."

Linnea figured it would have to be some major luck if Tammy left anything that would lead them to Gideon's current location. Still, it was worth a try.

Bryce volleyed some glances at Jace and her, and Linnea thought that meant he had something else on his mind. And she was right.

"I've arranged for a safe house for Linnea," he finally said to Jace. "In fact, I think it would be a good idea to take her there now. That way, she can stay out of Zimmerman's way while I work on killing any warrant he might have managed to get. It's the smart thing to do, what with Gideon after her."

"Gideon's after Jace, too," Linnea quickly pointed out.

Bryce nodded. "But Jace is a cop and can take care of himself. I'm not so sure he can take care of you right now." He sighed when she just stared at him. "Linnea, this isn't a personal offer. It's something I feel I need to do. I owe you," he amended. "If I'd uncovered Gideon's dirty dealings sooner, he'd be behind bars, and you wouldn't be in danger."

"Maybe," she agreed in a mumble. She added some volume to her voice, though, when she continued. "But even with Gideon in jail, hurt or incapacitated, I'd still be in danger because none of us believes that my brother was acting alone. Whoever got to Toby could get to me."

"And that's my point," Bryce practically snapped. "You're a target here. You need to be in a safe house."

She glanced at Jace, who'd stayed quiet through all of this. A huge surprise, since he usually had an opinion on such things. But he hadn't needed to voice this particular opinion for her to know where he stood. Jace and she were of one mind when it came to this.

"Thank you, but no," she told Bryce. "I won't be

going to a safe house." At least not one that he'd arranged for her.

Bryce's mouth didn't exactly drop open, but his expression showed his surprise. "I'm offering you a chance at safety. A chance to live."

"Yeah, I got that," Linnea told him, "but I'd rather take my chances here with Jace."

"Jace is hurt," Bryce snapped. "He can't protect you if someone comes barging in here."

Linnea shrugged and tried to look totally unbothered by the fact that what he'd said might be true. "Jace protected me just fine when we were in the woods and a sniper tried to take us out." She paused, met his gaze head-on. "I'm not going to a safe house with you," she repeated.

Bryce threw sharp glances at them again, but this time his eyes were slightly narrowed. "Okay. Fine." He opened his mouth, closed it and then shook his head. "The offer stands if you change your mind."

With that, Bryce turned and walked out. Or rather, he stormed out. He was obviously riled that she hadn't taken him up on his plan.

"I'll head back to the office and see if there are any updates," Glenn muttered, stepping out.

Linnea looked down at Jace and realized that he'd slid his hand over the gun in the backpack. "I take it that you didn't want me to go with Bryce?"

"No, I didn't," he said right off. "I don't trust him. Actually, there aren't many people I trust right now."

"I hear you," she muttered. "My list of people I trust is pretty short and has just one name on it. Yours. Maybe Glenn's, too, but for right now, it's just you."

"Put Glenn's on the list," he advised. "The rest of my deputies, too." Jace looked away, cursed. "Bryce was right about one thing, though. I might not be able to fight off someone who breaks in."

This wasn't a pity party. Jace wasn't the kind of guy who indulged in self-pity. And both of them knew there was truth to what he'd just said.

"You might not be able to save me," she admitted. "Then again, maybe no one can. Or heck, maybe I can save myself and you."

Because she wanted to lighten the mood some, Linnea flexed her arms and motioned toward the slightly ripped muscles there. Slightly. He looked at her, but there was no lightening of his mood.

"Am I going to have to talk about that kiss in the barn again to distract you?" she teased.

His hand reached out, extremely fast for someone recovering from a gunshot wound. He took hold of her wrist, drew her down to him, and he very much distracted her by kissing her.

Linnea definitely hadn't seen that coming, and the feeling of his mouth on hers nearly knocked her off her feet. It robbed her of any common sense, too, because she forgot all about the danger. Forgot about her brother. Heck, she forgot how to breathe. But, man, oh man, she could taste and feel.

There it was. That trickle of heat, like warm honey making its way from her mouth to the rest of her. Making her tingle. Making her want things that she was certain Jace could give her. Linnea wasn't sure how Jace could manage such things with only some lip-to-lip contact. Then again, this was Jace. He had her number when it came to such things.

He didn't deepen this kiss. Didn't use his tongue or touch her except for the grip he had on her wrist. And that grip just melted away when he leaned back, and she stared into those stormy gray eyes.

Jace didn't say a word. He just stared at her, clearly waiting for her reaction. Of course, he could see her flushed face. Could hear her ragged breathing. Could almost certainly see the pulse throbbing in her throat, and he would know that the rest of her was doing some throbbing, too.

"Did that distract you?" he asked.

Except he didn't just ask, he drawled it. Hotshot was back. But the attitude didn't last long. It vanished as quickly as it'd come. Jace laid his head back on the bed and looked as if he wanted to curse as he had when Bryce had been there.

"A distraction isn't a good thing right now," he spelled out for her. "I need to be working on the investigation."

Linnea resisted saying something along the lines

of *No, it wasn't a good thing, but the kiss was amazing.* It had been. Both amazing and incredibly hot. Instead, she reached into the backpack and took out the laptop. Best to put the kiss aside and forget that it had happened.

Or rather try to forget.

She was reasonably sure she'd remember it for the rest of her life. Ditto for the first one he'd given her. But what might be the hardest for her to forget was the future kisses that she very much wanted from him.

"Since typing might be hard on your arm," she said, "I can do whatever computer searches you need."

He stared at her for a moment. Maybe because he was having that whole forgetting problem, too, but Jace finally nodded.

"Send Glenn an email," he instructed. "His name and addy are in my contacts. Ask him to do a full background on Tammy. I want to know everything about her, and if SAPD hasn't put a BOLO on her, I want that done, too."

While Linnea was pulling up that info, she considered something. "If Tammy isn't with Gideon, she could be dead. Gideon might be tying up any loose ends." And a woman who was privy to his crimes would indeed qualify as a loose end.

Jace nodded so fast that it was obviously something he'd already considered. "It's possible, but if so, Gideon managed to cover some ground fast. Toby's here in Culver Crossing, and according to Bryce, Tammy's house is in San Antonio. Of course, Gideon or his partner could have had Tammy meet them somewhere."

True, and Tammy might not have realized her loose-end status until it'd been too late. Still, if what they feared hadn't happened, and they managed to find the woman, she could perhaps tell them the identity of Gideon's partner and Gideon's whereabouts. The DA might be willing to make her a deal in exchange for info that could bring down a dirty cop and a criminal operation.

Linnea fired off the email to Glenn and turned to Jace to get instructions on what she should do next, when there was a knock at the door. A moment later, the security guard peered in.

"Sheriff Castillo," the guard said. "You got a visitor, and he says it's real important."

"Who is it?" Jace asked, and he slid his hand over his gun again.

"It's me," their visitor said, and even though Linnea wasn't that familiar with his voice, she still recognized him.

Zimmerman.

The agent stepped around the guard and flashed his badge. His gaze zoomed right to Linnea.

"Miss Martell." Zimmerman whipped out her name. "You need to come with me now."

Chapter Seven

Even though Jace was nowhere near steady, he got out of the bed, standing in front of Linnea. He also drew his gun.

That didn't cool down the hot anger in Zimmerman's eyes.

"Do I need to give you a closer look at my badge?" Zimmerman snarled at Jace. "Do I need to remind you that I'm an ATF agent and that you ran out on me at the cabin when I was trying to help you?"

"ATF agents can be dirty, just like cops," Jace pointed out. "Linnea's brother almost certainly has a partner, and since I don't know you, it could be you."

That didn't help with the anger, either. Muscles tightened and flexed in Zimmerman's jaw. Jace figured the same thing was happening on his own face. He was sick and tired of dealing with badge slingers that he wasn't sure he could trust.

"I'm taking her into custody," Zimmerman insisted. "At best she's a material witness to her brother's crimes. At worst, she's working with him. I intend to find out which."

Linnea started to move out from behind Jace, probably because she wanted to look Zimmerman in the eye to return some verbal fire. Jace was all for verbal fire, but Zimmerman was armed, and if he pulled that standard-issue Glock, then Jace wanted himself between the agent and her. That was why Jace shifted—causing him enough pain to make him have to bite back a grimace—so that he was in front of her again.

"At best, you have a boatload of speculation about Linnea," Jace shot back at the agent. "At worst, your intentions, whether good or bad, could get her killed. The second she walks out of this hospital, someone could try to gun her down."

He heard Linnea's slight shiver of breath. She'd already no doubt considered this, but it was likely a kick to the teeth to hear it spelled out like that.

"Considering I'm not a patient in the hospital, I can protect her a lot better than you can," Zimmerman argued. He motioned for Linnea to step out. "You're coming with me."

"She's not." Jace didn't raise his voice, but the hard stare he gave Zimmerman let him know this was not up for negotiation.

Since Bryce had just left the hospital only minutes earlier, he probably hadn't had time to learn anything that would help put a stop to Zimmerman. But Jace wasn't going to wait for Bryce to lend a hand.

Zimmerman huffed. "She can help me find her brother. She can put an end to this just by cooperating with me."

"Clearly, I have a different opinion about that," Jace countered.

"I don't know where Gideon is," Linnea spoke up, and much to Jace's frustration, she stepped around him so they were side by side. "If I did, I would have already told Jace. I trust him," she added after pausing a heartbeat. "I don't trust you. No offense. But right now, your badge is a huge negative."

"You don't have a choice," Zimmerman insisted, and he took a step toward her. "I'm taking you into custody."

"Enough of this," Jace growled. "Show me your warrant, and then I can start the calls to get it blocked."

That stopped the agent in his tracks, and even though he wasn't quick to admit it, Zimmerman's narrowed eyes told Jace what he needed to know.

There was no warrant.

"Without a warrant, you have no grounds to take Linnea," Jace added, and he tried not to sound too smug about that.

Oh, that didn't please Zimmerman. "I'll have a warrant by morning."

"Then, you can come back, and I'll start those calls to block it," Jace said just as fast.

"And in the meantime, her brother is as free as a

bird." Zimmerman flung an accusing finger at Linnea. "If she'd just cooperate, we could get him off the streets so he can't go after someone else. You of all people should know that, since Gideon's the one who shot you."

Jace shrugged. Regretted it. Oh, man. He really needed to do some fast healing. "I'm well aware of who shot me. Well aware, too, that you're on a fishing expedition to help bolster your investigation. Linnea isn't going on that expedition with you."

"Tomorrow she will," Zimmerman snapped.

"Then come back tomorrow when you have the warrant," Jace *invited*. In the meantime, he'd go ahead and start those calls to block Zimmerman in any way he could. If the calls failed, Jace would get her out of the agent's reach.

And yeah, that wasn't just bending the law. It was breaking it.

Still, having her stay with him was his best shot at keeping her alive.

"Uh, boss," someone said from the door. It was Deputy Crystal Rankin, and she was giving Zimmerman the hard eye. She also set a large leather bag on the floor and rested her hand on the butt of her service weapon. "Is there a problem?"

"No," Jace assured her, though his body language no doubt indicated otherwise. "Agent Zimmerman was just leaving."

Despite Jace's tone of "don't let the door hit you

in the ass on the way out," Zimmerman didn't budge. He stood there, shifting his gaze from Linnea, to Jace, then to Crystal. He definitely noted the way Crystal had now gripped her gun, and he must have decided that this wasn't a fight he was going to win.

"You can't block this," Zimmerman said to Jace, and it sounded like a warning. "This investigation is under my jurisdiction now."

"Really. *Yours*?" Jace challenged. "What about San Antonio PD? Seems they'd want to go after one of their own."

Plus, there was the part about Toby being killed in Culver Crossing. Toby might have been a screw-up, but he definitely qualified as one of Jace's own.

"SAPD is running their own Internal Affairs investigation, but this is now a federal case. My case," Zimmerman said like he was speaking gospel. "You'll be getting official word on that very soon."

Zimmerman didn't seem to be bluffing about that, so Jace settled for saying, "All right. But without a warrant, you're leaving. If you refuse, my deputy and the security guard will escort you from the building."

As expected, the agent didn't like any of that. Also as expected, Zimmerman tried to intimidate him with a stare down. It didn't work. Jace kept up his own stare and motioned for Crystal and the guard to get Zimmerman out of there. Crystal reached for the agent's arm, but Zimmerman threw off her attempted grip with far more force than necessary.

"I'll be back," Zimmerman said. That was a warning, too. But he finally turned to leave.

Jace heard Linnea release the breath that she'd no doubt been holding too long, and they watched until Zimmerman was out of sight. Only then did Crystal shut the door. Only then did Jace get back in the bed. It was best not to risk a slam to his dignity by falling on his butt.

"You want me to have him followed, to make sure he leaves the hospital?" Crystal asked.

He considered it and shook his head. "He'll leave, and maybe now he knows he can't just walk in here."

Jace was also hoping that Linnea and he wouldn't be in this room much longer. He needed to get out so he could take her someplace where people he didn't trust couldn't get close to her.

Crystal nodded but cast an uneasy glance at the windows. Jace had done the same himself, a little while ago. The blinds were down, but it wouldn't take much for someone to figure out what room he was in and start blasting. That was yet another reason to take Linnea elsewhere.

But where?

That was the million-dollar question, and he didn't have an answer yet. That was something else he had to work out before morning, because one way or another, that was when Linnea and he would be leaving the hospital.

"I'll be standing guard outside your door for a while," Crystal explained. "Bennie will relieve me at midnight."

Bennie Waterman was another of his deputies, one with a ton of experience and a level head. Ditto for Crystal. Glenn had chosen well when he'd worked up the schedule for guard duty.

"No one gets in here without you asking me first," Jace emphasized.

Crystal gave another nod, and she made a sound to indicate that was understood. "The CSIs finished up at Toby's a little while ago," she said. "They found some blood on the knob of the back door. The lock had been compromised, so that's how we think the killer gained access to the house."

Jace had yet to see photos of the crime scene, but he suspected that because of the manner of death, there would be lots of blood in and around Toby's body. It was highly likely that some of that blood had gotten on the killer, and he or she had transferred some to that knob on the way out.

"The blood was on both the front and the back of the knob," Crystal added. "There was also blood inside the lock, maybe transferred there when the intruder picked it."

Well, that caused Jace to amend his theory and hinted at another possibility. One that could be a huge break in the investigation. The blood inside the lock could mean the person who'd entered had already been bleeding. If it wasn't Gideon's partner or hired gun who'd killed Toby, then Gideon himself could have done the deed.

"It could be the killer's blood," Linnea concluded after glancing at Crystal and him. "It could be Gideon's."

"Could be," Jace agreed, and he looked up at Crystal. "Light a fire under the lab to make sure it gets processed ASAP."

"I will. I brought my laptop with me so I could get some work done." The deputy picked up the leather bag that she'd set on the floor when she'd seen Zimmerman, and tipped her head to the windows. "Now that I'm relieving the security guard, I'll ask him to patrol the grounds. That might discourage someone from trying to get close."

It might, and Jace gave her the go-ahead nod, along with a thank-you as Crystal left the room.

"You shot Gideon," Linnea said once Crystal had shut the door. "But he'd know better than to leave a trace of himself on that doorknob or inside the lock. Or anywhere else in the house, for that matter." She stopped and some of the color drained from her face.

"What's wrong?" he immediately asked.

Linnea held up her left hand, and he saw the small bandage just below the base of her fingers. "Day before yesterday, I cut myself when I was opening a bag of mulch. The job was near Gideon's place, so I went there to get cleaned up. I wiped away some blood with some paper towels, cleaned up and threw the bloody towels in the trash."

"Gideon was there?" Jace wanted to know.

"Yes. He's the one who handed me the paper towel roll so I could tear off some sheets." She looked a little ill when she sank onto the side of the bed next to him. "The cut wasn't bad, but there was blood." Linnea paused. "That happened the day before I found out what he'd been doing."

She didn't have to ask the question that was on her mind. Jace had followed this through to one possible conclusion.

A bad one.

That Gideon had used those paper towels to plant her blood on the doorknob and inside the lock. If so, it meant that after Jace had shot him, Gideon could have gone back to his house to get the bloody paper towels. Or maybe Gideon had had someone retrieve them to be used at Toby's. Either way, it could be Linnea's DNA that turned up when the lab ran the tests.

Hell.

"This could give Zimmerman ammunition to get that warrant for my arrest," Linnea muttered.

It could, but Jace could still argue that this was a setup, that Linnea had been with him in the cabin when Toby was murdered a good twenty miles away. That was why he needed to press the medical examiner to get a more exact time of death. It could be critical info in fighting Zimmerman.

And that led Jace to something they needed to consider.

"If things don't go our way with Zimmerman," he said, "you and I might have to take a trip."

She stayed quiet a moment. "We might have to go into hiding."

It twisted at him to consider this because the bottom line was that it would mean breaking the law. He believed in upholding the law, but it wouldn't be justice to hand Linnea over to a federal agent who could allow her to be murdered.

Jace held her gaze a moment longer, silently letting her know that yes, they'd go into hiding if Zimmerman gave them no other choice. Maybe, though, he could find another ATF agent, one he trusted. He didn't like the fact that Zimmerman had shown up at the cabin so soon after the shooting. And that Zimmerman was pushing so hard to try to take Linnea into custody. Maybe he was just doing his job, but Jace had to consider the agent might be trying to get Linnea into a position where he could silence her.

He took out his phone to get started on finding another ATF agent, but before he could make a call, it rang.

Apparently, Glenn had transferred Jace's contacts to this replacement phone, because the deputy's name popped up on the screen.

"Boss," Glenn said the moment Jace answered. "Gideon's been sighted."

Since the situation with Zimmerman was still in his head, it took a moment for that to sink in, and Jace put the call on speaker so that Linnea could hear. This was definitely something she'd want to know.

"Where?" Jace asked.

Oh, yes, she wanted to know. She not only moved closer, but Linnea also pulled in her breath.

"On a security camera outside a convenience store in Bulverde," Glenn explained.

That was about twenty miles away. Not far at all.

"You're sure it's Gideon?" Jace pressed.

"Positive. Gideon called the sheriff's office about twenty minutes ago and said I should check the feed from that particular security camera. The store manager cooperated and sent it to me right away." Glenn paused. "Boss, it's something you're gonna want to see. I'm sending it to your laptop now."

Jace put his phone aside so he could take the laptop, and sure enough, the moment he checked his messages, he spotted the video file that Glenn had just emailed him. The deputy had apparently done the work of going through the feed so it started with a man moving into camera range. A man wearing a black San Antonio Spurs cap and dark sunglasses.

It was Gideon.

Linnea made a slight gasp, and judging from the muttered profanity that followed, it was a sound that she wished she'd managed to stifle. It had to be a shock to see the face of a brother who wanted her dead, but she had probably hoped she'd steeled herself up better by now. Jace was thinking there wasn't enough steeling in the world for her to see that face.

"He's alive," Linnea said under her breath.

Yeah, he was.

Jace froze the frame and zoomed in, checking Gideon for any signs of a gunshot wound. He certainly wasn't bloody or hunched in pain, but he was wearing a bulky windbreaker, outerwear that wasn't needed since they weren't in the middle of a storm. So Gideon might have used the windbreaker to cover up a bandage. Or it could be that Jace had been wrong, and he hadn't managed to shoot him after all.

He hit the play function again, and Jace watched as Gideon looked straight up at the camera. In the same motion, the man pulled a sheet of paper from inside the windbreaker.

"Something's written on it," Linnea quickly pointed out.

He'd noticed that, too, and was already zooming in. There were only five words, followed by ten numbers, but they were written so large that they took up almost the entire sheet of paper.

"Jace, we have to talk," Linnea read loud, and she repeated the numbers that Gideon had on the makeshift sign he was holding.

"A phone number," Jace mumbled.

"Yes, but it's not Gideon's number. Well, not his

usual one. But he's probably using a burner cell so his location can't be tracked."

That was Jace's bet, too.

"Please tell me cops were sent to this location," Jace said to Glenn on the phone.

"They were. They're on the way now," Glenn assured him. "I'm guessing, though, that Gideon won't be there."

"No," Jace agreed, "but let me give him a call and see what he has to say. I'll record the conversation and send it to you to be analyzed."

He ended the call with Glenn, and once he had the recorder function on, Jace quickly pressed in the numbers that had been on the sign. Since it rang, it was indeed a phone number. A working one, because on the fourth ring, the call transferred to a message.

"Jace," the message said. Definitely Gideon's voice. "I've been set up. I had to say what I said to you in the woods. If I hadn't, we would have both been executed on the spot."

He glanced at Linnea to see how she was reacting, and she had the same skeptical look that Jace was certain was on his own face.

"In a day or two, I'll call you with a time and a place for a meeting," Gideon went on. "I have proof I'm innocent, and I'll give it to you then. In the meantime, protect my sister. Because, Jace, Linnea is the reason all of this is happening."

Chapter Eight

Linnea is the reason all of this is happening.

Though she'd tried to tell herself that her brother's message was an attempt to muddy the investigation, Linnea hadn't been able to push the possibility of it aside. It was one of the reasons that she hadn't gotten much sleep. That, and the fact that she had spent the night in a recliner right next to Jace.

He'd occupied plenty of her thoughts, too.

Those thoughts proved she was off-kilter. Way off. Even the threat of danger hanging over them hadn't stopped her from remembering that Jace and she would no doubt be sharing tight quarters for a while. Tight quarters that certainly wouldn't give her space to recover from the effect he was having on her.

Like now, for instance.

It was barely past six in the morning, a time that Jace had decided was when they needed to leave the hospital. He'd already spoken to the nurses about getting Dr. Garcia in to sign his release papers. He had also set up transportation with his deputies and asked them to secure her house—where they'd be going until he could come up with another solution.

The temporary solution caused her stomach to jitter some. After all, someone had broken into her house and stolen the knife used in Toby's murder. Still, it made more sense to go there than to Jace's. His ranch was outside of town, and her place wasn't that far from the sheriff's office. The deputies would be able to get there in minutes if there was a problem.

Unfortunately, it might take a killer less than minutes to finish them off.

To ready himself for their departure, which Jace apparently thought would happen very soon, he'd already managed to remove his hospital gown and was attempting to dress himself in the clothes that Glenn had brought over the day before. That meant he was naked.

Well, mostly.

While sitting on the edge of his bed, he'd gotten on his boxers while she pretended she was blind, but he was struggling with the jeans. On a sigh, Linnea ditched the blindness pretense and went to him.

"You know," she muttered, "this is going to give me inappropriate thoughts about you."

She caught onto the waist of his jeans and pulled them up. And yep, there were indeed some inappropriate thoughts. Some touching, too. Linnea tried not to notice all the interesting parts of him. Of course, everything about Jace was interesting.

When she zipped him up, she lifted her head and collided with his gaze. He was watching her, and he appeared to be fighting a smile. Of all the reactions he could have had, that wasn't an especially bad one. It was better than pain. Or heat.

But it didn't last.

The heat came when his gaze dropped to her mouth. He didn't kiss her, but it made her wish he would. Instead, he did the responsible thing and looked away. He reached for a blue button-up shirt, but Linnea didn't even let him attempt that on his own. Not with that huge bandage on his shoulder. She got his good arm in the sleeve and got to work easing on the shirt on the other side.

"Linnea is the reason all of this is happening," she said, repeating what Gideon had told them in that recorded message.

Reminding Jace of that was a distraction ploy because she knew all the moving around had to be painful, but she also did want to open up another discussion about it. When she'd tried the night before, all she'd gotten from Jace was a growled, "Gideon is the reason all of this is happening."

Jace looked up at her, repeated his words from the night before. He added, "This isn't your fault."

Linnea wanted to believe that. She truly did, but it was yet something else to eat away at her.

"No one was holding a gun to Gideon's head when he ran from me," Jace went on. "No one went into those woods with us. If someone had been with him, I would have seen or heard something."

That was true. But there was something else she wanted him to consider.

"The person wouldn't have had to be there to threaten me," she suggested. "Playing devil's advocate here, but what if someone else threatened to kill me, and that's the reason Gideon stole those guns and drugs?"

There was no way Jace's look could have gotten any flatter or be filled with any more skepticism. However, he didn't call her an idiot for considering that. He just sighed.

"He's your brother, and he probably wants you to have doubts about his guilt," Jace explained. "That way, he can get close enough to finish us off."

But then he paused. Cursed. And he shook his head.

"Trust me," Jace said, looking her straight in the eyes, "if there's a chance Gideon has been set up or forced to do these crimes, I'll find out."

"I do trust you." Linnea didn't have a single doubt about that.

"But?" he challenged.

"No but." She finished getting his arm into the shirt and began to button it. "I just wish, well, I just wish," she settled for saying.

He nodded, stared at her for a moment, and then finally broke the eye contact so he could tip his head toward his boots.

"Help me with those," he said, "and maybe we can get out of here before Zimmerman or Bryce show up."

She certainly hadn't forgotten about those two. Zimmerman just might have that arrest warrant with him. As for Bryce, if he was truly a dirty cop, then he could make a return visit to try to figure out the best way to go after them.

While Linnea helped Jace put on his boots, she also glanced up at him. This time, though, it was to see if he was in as much pain as he had been the night before. Maybe. But if so, he was doing a better job of covering it up.

"What if Dr. Garcia won't discharge you?" she asked.

"I'm leaving whether he does or not." Jace took a shoulder holster from the backpack. He must have realized he wouldn't be able to get it on with his injury, so he put it away and instead slipped his gun into the back waist of his jeans.

Getting ready in case they were attacked.

It was only a couple of blocks from the hospital to her house, but it was also broad daylight. A sniper might try to pick them off. She got such a clear image of that happening that it was probably why she nearly jumped when there was a knock at the door.

"It's me," Glenn said from the other side. The deputy raised an eyebrow when he came in and spotted Jace already dressed. "You okay, boss?"

"Fine," Jace said and didn't even pause before he jumped right in. "Update me on the investigation."

Glenn nodded as if he'd expected to do just that. "The lab folks aren't real happy with us, but I got them to put our evidence at the top of the heap." He looked at Linnea. "It was your blood on the doorknob and in the lock at Toby's house."

She didn't come close to jumping this time, because it was exactly what she had expected him to say. Still, it stung—especially if Gideon had been the one to do this.

"I had a CSI go over to Gideon's and check to see if there were any signs of bloody paper towels in the trash," Glenn went on. "Nothing. But they are going to test the trash can. If there are any traces of your blood in it, then it'll back up your statement."

Linnea huffed. She apparently needed such things to prove her innocence. Of course, Jace didn't believe she was guilty, so he was on her side.

"I didn't send Zimmerman or anybody else a copy of the lab report," Glenn explained. "If it comes up, I'll just say we got so busy what with you out on medical that I forgot to copy them."

"Good," Jace mumbled, and he showed some signs of weariness when he scrubbed his hand over his face. "What about the feed from the security camera at the convenience store?" he asked. "Did the lab guys get to study that?"

"Only a quick glance, but I had a good look at it, and I enlarged a couple of the images and printed them out for you." Glenn pulled two photographs from an envelope he was carrying and handed them to Jace.

Linnea hurried to Jace's side to study them. The man was definitely her brother, but then she hadn't had any doubts about that. In one image he was reaching inside his windbreaker, and Linnea didn't think it was the overhead street light that made him look so pale. Plus, his face was sweaty. Not the kind of perspiration from a hot night, either. He looked hurt, and his forehead was bunched up as if wincing.

"I was pretty sure I'd shot him," Jace remarked. "Guess I was right."

Yes, and it made her wonder if Gideon had gotten medical care. There would have been alerts at the hospitals in case he showed up at one of them, but he probably had friends with enough training to help him out. After all, she'd been the one who'd tended Jace's injuries.

Jace moved on to the second picture, and in this one, Gideon had moved back the windbreaker even further to take out the sign. And she saw it. The blood on his shirt.

"He's hurt but mobile," Jace said, studying the

picture. "Or faking an injury to make us believe he's not as much of a threat."

Linnea hadn't gone there yet, but she would have worked her way around to it. Everything Gideon did right now was suspect.

Glenn took out some other papers from the envelope and gave them to Jace. "That's for Linnea's order of protective custody. You said you wanted that on file in case Zimmerman came in and demanded that she go with him."

Linnea hadn't heard that particular request, but she had been aware that Jace and Glenn had emailed and texted many, many times since Jace's arrival at the hospital. Jace glanced over the papers, took the pen that Glenn offered him and signed it.

"That'll hold up against a warrant?" she asked.

Glenn shrugged. "It's something we can take to a judge to maybe stop you from being transferred to ATF custody."

She didn't like that *maybe*. And that brought her to another concern. "Zimmerman could just show up at my house."

"He could," Glenn quickly agreed, "but the idea is to stop him before he gets that far."

Linnea nearly asked what happened if they didn't stop him from getting that far, but she would just have to trust Jace and Glenn on this. And keep her own gun ready. If it hadn't been stolen or confiscated during the CSI search, she had a snub-nosed

.38 in her closet. Ironically, it was one that Gideon had given to her years ago.

Jace handed the signed protection order and photos back to Glenn. "What about a time of death on Toby? Do you have one yet from the medical examiner?"

"Night before last, around midnight," Glenn readily answered. "When Linnea was with you."

Yes, she had been, but with Jace unconscious, he wouldn't have known that for certain.

"She was with me," Jace verified. "And what about Tammy? Anything new on her?"

Glenn's face brightened a little. "Yes. One of Tammy's neighbors said the lights were on in her apartment late last night, and he called SAPD because he knew they were looking for her. However, before the cops could show up, the neighbor said someone came out carrying a suitcase. He was pretty sure it was Tammy."

So the woman was alive. Too bad the cops hadn't gotten there a little sooner, and they could have taken her for questioning. Then again, if Bryce was dirty, he might have made sure Tammy never got the chance to be interrogated.

"Was anyone with Tammy?" Jace asked, and Linnea knew he meant Gideon.

"No, not that the neighbor saw, but he said it's possible someone was waiting for her in her car. It was dark, and she hadn't parked in her usual space in front of her door. She'd left her car at the edge of the parking lot where there isn't much light."

No way had Tammy done that by chance, so maybe she had been trying to conceal whoever had been in the vehicle. Though it was possible she was just trying to sneak in and out without anyone noticing. Plenty of people, including cops, could have seen her walking across a parking lot. After all, Bryce had said he intended to get a warrant to search Tammy's place.

Jace stayed quiet a moment, obviously giving that some thought. "It would have been stupid for Gideon to go there with her."

It would have been, but maybe Gideon had risked it if Tammy had needed to get something important from her apartment. Perhaps money or cash. Or weapons.

There was a quick knock at the door, and as he'd done before, Jace automatically stepped in front of her. Glenn pivoted, too, and took the stance of a lawman about to draw his gun. But it wasn't a threat. It was Dr. Garcia who came walking in.

The doctor took one look at Jace and frowned. Then he sighed as if in resignation. "Will it do any good whatsoever to tell you that you need another day of bed rest?" Dr. Garcia asked.

"None," Jace answered without hesitation. "I'm leaving." He shifted his attention to Glenn. "Is the cruiser ready to take Linnea and me?"

"It is," Glenn replied. "You want me to move it closer to the exit doors?"

"I do. Linnea and I will be out in just a few minutes."

That was no doubt Jace's way of telling the doctor that he wasn't going to wait around, and that was probably why Dr. Garcia sighed again.

"Okay." The doctor scribbled something on Jace's chart. "I'll phone in a script for some pain meds. Linnea, will you be able to check the wound and redress it the way you did before Jace got to the hospital?"

She nodded, though she wondered if she should say no and try to talk Jace into staying put a little longer. "Is it safe for Jace to leave?" she asked. "Will it cause some damage for him to move around?"

"Not necessarily damage, but it'll slow the healing process." The doctor scrawled something else on a notepad and handed it to her. "That's my cell number if you have any questions about the wound or the meds."

"I won't be taking the meds," Jace insisted.

The doctor looked resigned to that, too. "Then, at least take it easy and get plenty of rest."

Of course, everybody in the room, including the doctor, knew that wasn't going to happen. Once they got to her place, Jace would launch into what would turn out to be a long workday as he took up the investigation.

"I'll move the cruiser," Glenn said after the doctor walked out. "I'll text you when I'm ready."

Jace muttered a thank-you and began to gather up the things to put in the backpack. Here was something she could do to stop him from moving around too much, so she took the laptop from his and added it to the other items already in the bag. She'd barely gotten it zipped up when Jace's phone rang.

"That couldn't be Glenn already," she muttered. And it wasn't.

"It's me," the caller said the moment Jace answered.

Even though the phone wasn't on speaker, Linnea had no trouble hearing the voice.

Gideon.

Chapter Nine

A lot of emotions went through Jace when he heard his old friend's voice, but the trust he'd once gotten from their friendship wasn't one of them. Despite what Gideon had said about being set up, Jace had some serious doubts.

"Where are you?" Jace asked him, and he hit the record function on his phone so he could go over every bit of this conversation later.

Of course, Gideon didn't jump to answer that. He not only paused for several moments, but Jace also thought he heard another voice. One murmuring in the background. Of course, that could be part of the ruse. If a ruse was indeed what Gideon had in mind. Or maybe Tammy was with him, though Jace couldn't tell if it was a man's or woman's voice.

"I need to set up a meeting with you," Gideon continued long seconds later. "We have to talk."

"So you said last night when you called." Jace didn't bother to take the sarcasm out of his tone. "Do you really believe I'm going to meet you and give you the chance to try to kill me again?"

"Hey, I'm risking the same thing," Gideon fired back. "You could use this meeting to gun me down, too. I just need to give you some proof that I'm innocent, and it has to be done face-to-face."

Jace huffed, but before he answered Gideon, he shot a quick glance at Linnea. As he'd expected, she was hanging on every word. Like Jace, she was probably trying to analyze everything she was hearing. Thankfully, what she wasn't doing was making any attempt to try to talk to her brother. No way did Jace want to confirm to Gideon that Linnea was with him.

"You said Linnea is the reason all of this is happening," Jace reminded Gideon. "What the hell does it mean?"

He heard Gideon take a deep breath. "I think it goes back to Bryce. Things ended badly between them, and I think it caused something to snap."

Jace huffed and rolled his eyes. "Because Linnea wouldn't keep dating him?" And yep, he added even more sarcasm. "That's the reason a cop would commit a laundry list of crimes?"

Gideon gave a huff of his own. "Bryce had a thing for Linnea for years, and when she went out with him a couple of times, he thought it was going to be the start of something big. The start of their future together."

It sounded like a crock to Jace, but again he

glanced at Linnea to see if she thought that theory was even in the realm of being possible. She shrugged. Definitely not a flag-waving declaration of Bryce's innocence.

Hell.

A lieutenant in SAPD could have definitely set up something like this. Could possibly be pulling the strings even now. But then Jace remembered the taunts Gideon had tossed out during their gunfight.

"To hell with Linnea. She's the one who ratted me out," Jace repeated. "That's what you said. And more. You also said, as far as you were concerned, Linnea could die right along with me."

"I was wired," Gideon insisted, "and the person who set me up was giving me messages, telling me what to say."

Jace jumped right on that. "If you were getting messages, then you know if it's Bryce or not."

"No. He was disguising his voice. But I believe it was Bryce," Gideon quickly added. "That's why we have to meet, so I can give you what I have."

"And what is it exactly that you have?" Jace snapped.

"Statements from CIs—"

"You mean from Tammy?" Jace interrupted.

Gideon paused. Or maybe it was a hesitation as he tried to figure out the right way to spin this. "Yes, from her and others. I've got statements from three people who say I wasn't part of the illegal operation."

As Linnea had done earlier, Jace didn't bother to point out the criminal part of the CI's title. "You'd better have more than the hearsay of CIs."

"I do. I have the login sheet for one of the warehouses where I supposedly took some guns. I have an alibi for that time."

Jace groaned but also tried to listen to the background sounds. No more mutterings. No sounds of traffic or machinery, either. "Let me guess—Tammy is your alibi?"

"She is." There was some defiance in Gideon's voice now. "But I have a receipt for the dinner we had. I can give all of this to you when we meet."

There was no *when* to this. "Why meet with me?" Jace challenged. "If you're truly innocent as you say you are, send the evidence to San Antonio PD, and they can deal with it."

Gideon didn't pause this time. "Bryce has friends throughout the force. I don't know whom I can trust there."

Jace wanted to curse and tell Gideon exactly what he thought of this idiotic demand for a meeting. But more than that, he needed information from Gideon. For starters, his location. Then, his partner or partners in crime. He seriously doubted that Gideon was just going to volunteer that, so Jace intended to keep him talking.

"How'd Bryce set you up?" Jace asked.

This time, Gideon didn't hesitate. "By duplicating my badge and using a disguise to get into those warehouses to steal the guns and weapons."

"Convenient," Jace muttered. "I haven't been able to confirm who tried to set up your sister, but that's exactly what her accuser claimed she'd done."

"Not Linnea." Gideon's voice was barely audible this time, but it sounded as if there was some regret or maybe doubt in his voice. "She's in danger, Jace. She needs to be protected."

Linnea opened her mouth, but before she could say anything, Jace shook his head to silence her— even though he knew it had to be hard for her just to stand there and listen to this.

Jace's phone dinged with a text from Glenn, letting him know that he was ready with the cruiser, but Jace didn't want to have this conversation as Linnea and he walked through the hospital. He wanted to be on full alert because it was entirely possible that this call was meant to distract them to make it easier for Gideon or a hired gun to murder them. Jace sent a quick text to Glenn to let him know they'd be out soon.

"You can't trace this call," Gideon said. He'd apparently heard the clicks of the text. "I'm using a burner."

"So I figured." Jace decided to move this along because there was another possibility for things to go wrong here. Gideon could be using this as a stall tactic to keep Linnea and him in the hospital room so someone could shoot through the window.

Damned if they did, and damned if they didn't.

"Let's assume I might be interested in meeting with you," Jace continued. "When and where would this take place?"

"Today. This morning if possible. The sooner the better," Gideon added so fast that his words ran together.

"All right," Jace said. "Meet me in my office in one hour."

Gideon laughed, but there was definitely no humor in it. "I'm not going to make it easy for you to kill or arrest me. I don't trust you any more than you trust me."

Finally, he was certain Gideon had spoken the truth. "Yet you want to meet with me," Jace reminded him.

"I *have* to meet with you," Gideon emphasized. "I have to give you this evidence so you can start clearing my name. It's the only way for Linnea and me to be safe."

Jace scowled over "the only way." He could do things to minimize Linnea being attacked again, but first and foremost, those things involved keeping her away from Gideon and his hired guns.

"When and where do you want to meet?" Jace pressed when Gideon didn't say anything else.

"I'll call you back with an exact time and location."

Yeah, and Jace was betting that time and location

would allow Gideon to set a trap. Or rather try to do that. So Jace turned the tables on him.

"Meet me in two hours at the place where I first kissed Linnea," Jace told Gideon.

As he'd expected, that got a reaction from Linnea. She pulled back her shoulders and stared at him as if he'd lost his mind. Gideon might have been doing the same thing, because he suddenly got very quiet.

"The barn at my family's ranch," Gideon finally muttered.

Bingo. Though Jace hadn't known that Gideon had been aware of that kiss or the location of it. Obviously, Linnea and he hadn't been as discreet about that as he'd thought.

"The place is empty," Jace reminded him. "There's no one around to get caught up in friendly fire if things go wrong."

That part was true. The ranch had literally been for sale for two years now, since Linnea's parents had been killed in an interstate collision while coming back from a vacation. Because both Linnea and Gideon already had their own places and hadn't wanted to live there, they'd put it up for sale.

"Swear to me that you won't just ambush me and gun me down," Gideon said.

Now it was Jace's turn to be surprised. "You'd take my word on that?" he asked.

"I would." Gideon sounded confident about that when Jace knew there was no way in hell he was.

Obviously, Gideon was willing to say whatever it took to get a second chance at tying up loose ends.

Maybe.

And it was that *maybe* that was eating away at Jace.

"I won't ambush you or gun you down," Jace promised. "But if it's a trap, then all bets are off."

"Deal," Gideon assured him. "But two hours won't work for me. I'll call you back with a time." And with that, he ended the call.

Jace stood there a moment, staring at the phone and wondering what the hell kind of game his former friend was playing.

"Come on," he told Linnea. "Let's get out of here before our luck runs out with Zimmerman."

Nodding, Linnea scooped up the backpack before Jace could, and she was right on his heels when he headed out. Crystal was just outside the door, obviously waiting for them.

"Glenn filled me in," the deputy said. "We can go this way to get to the cruiser."

This way was down the hall past the patients' rooms, past a nurse station and then into a waiting area. One that Glenn had cleared, from the looks of it, since there was no one around.

Good.

With fewer people, there'd be fewer distractions. Still, Jace continued to fire glances all around them as they made their way to the exit through the ER.

Glenn had pulled the cruiser practically up the sliding glass doors, and had even opened the back door so Linnea and he could just slide in. Linnea got in first and moved across the seat to make room for him. It took Jace a little longer, and he felt every movement and tug of the stitches in his shoulder. Hell. He needed to get past this pain fast.

"I had a couple of the reserve deputies go through Linnea's place," Glenn said when he drove away. "They're waiting there until you're tucked away inside and have the security system on."

That was the plan that Jace had gone over with Glenn the night before. Now Jace had to hope that it wasn't a stupid plan that would put Linnea and him in the sights of a killer.

"You believe Gideon?" Linnea asked him. It was a question that Jace had definitely expected. "You really think he has evidence to clear his name?"

"I think he has statements and such. I also think what he has isn't worth a thimble full of spit."

She made a sound of agreement and glanced away. But not before Jace saw something very dangerous in her eyes.

Hope.

Hope that her brother wasn't dirty, that this had indeed all been a setup. Jace didn't want her, or himself, thinking that way.

"Gideon wants to meet with me," Jace told Glenn, and he caught his deputy's surprised look as Glenn glanced in the rearview. "I told him I'd meet him at the barn on his parents' property."

"You won't go there," Glenn immediately said.

"I won't go there," Jace assured him. "Gideon probably won't, either. But he could have plans to have a sniper along the route." Jace stopped, rethought that. "Unless his game plan really is to try to convince me that he was set up. Either way, I won't be going to the barn."

"But what happens when Gideon calls back?" Linnea asked.

Jace still had plenty of things to work out about that, but he knew the gist of what he had to do. "I'll try to arrange to meet at another location, one where I can control the timing and the security. He probably won't go for it, but that would be the way I stand a chance of taking him into custody."

Linnea stayed quiet a moment, but like Jace, she was watching their surroundings. Unlike the ER waiting area, there were plenty of people out and about on Main Street. And yeah, some of those people had noticed him in the cruiser and would no doubt guess they were either going to Linnea's house or his. He wasn't sure though that any of the locals would share that info with Zimmerman or Bryce. There was plenty of gossip in Culver Crossing, but there was just as much distrust of outsiders.

"I need to work out a safe way for Gideon to get me copies of what he considers evidence to clear his

name," Jace went on when Glenn turned onto Bluebonnet Lane, the street where Linnea lived.

"Maybe I can help with that," she offered. "I
could talk to him and arrange for a meeting place
where he'll feel protected enough to show up. If
I'm there, he'll know it's not an ambush because
you wouldn't risk me being in the middle of possible gunfire."

He considered it, shook his head and then
shrugged. Nodded. No way would Linnea be part
of any meeting with Gideon, but maybe she could
go at her brother from a different angle than Jace
could. Through talk, not action. Blood ties could
maybe work better than friendship, and she might be
able to use those ties to get Gideon to show up so he
could then spill whatever it was he claimed he had.

Glenn slowed when they approached Linnea's
house. It was a single-story limestone-and-white
cottage with a much larger lot than what most other
residents had this close to Main Street. The houses,
including hers, were on several acres, which meant
there was plenty of space between her neighbors and
her. Plenty of landscaping, too.

She'd obviously turned her yard into a showcase
for customers.

There were pecan and oak trees mixed with
mountain laurels. The right mix. Everything looked
balanced, with the swirls of color in the flowers that
dotted the yard and curved around the stone walk-

way toward the porch. Jace had no idea what the flowers actually were, but there were beds of red, purple and white.

"The place looks good," he said, staring past the landscape to see any potential problem areas. There was a cluster of crepe myrtles that could turn out to be a hiding place for a gunman, and Jace made a mental note to keep Linnea away from the windows on that side of the house.

"Thanks. I haven't had a chance to weed in a while." She was no doubt seeing the work that needed to be done. Probably seeing the security pitfalls, too, because she added, "I have blackout shades we can pull down on the windows."

They'd definitely use those, and if they were still there come nightfall—which was highly likely— they wouldn't be turning on lights and advertising exactly where they were in the house.

Glenn pulled into Linnea's driveway and parked next to a cruiser that was already there. Jace immediately spotted the two reserve deputies on the porch. Darnell Hough and Manuel Rodriguez. Both had once been full-time deputies in the department but had retired. He trusted them, but Jace would check the place for himself to make sure they hadn't missed anything.

"The CSIs didn't break the door when they went in," Glenn explained. "In fact, they found the front door unlocked and the security system turned off."

Linnea's mouth tightened. "Whoever broke in to get the knife and earring probably did that. I always lock up the place tight, and I don't have a spare key hidden for someone to find."

Jace didn't doubt that, but at least this meant they'd have no trouble getting into her house now. He suspected she'd left her keys and purse at the cabin when she'd been trying to get them out on the ATV.

"You'll need to change the codes for the security system once we're inside," Jace reminded her and he got an immediate nod.

"I can do that on the panel box by the door," she assured him.

With all of them still keeping watch, Linnea and Jace hurried to the porch, and Jace took a moment to thank the reserve deputies before Linnea and he went inside. First things first, he locked the door and had her engage the security. Then, he went through the place room by room.

It wasn't an overly large house, but it was a decent size. A combination eating, living and dining area with three bedrooms and two baths. He knew the layout because he'd been here a couple of times. Once to help her move in and again when Gideon had brought him over for dinner.

Obviously, the CSIs had rifled through the place, leaving some cabinet doors and drawers open. On a sigh, Linnea set down the backpack and went to close them. Along the way, she started lowering the shades.

Jace lowered some, as well, while he made his way through the house, checking the locks on the windows and doors. He didn't have any trouble finding Linnea's bedroom. Or seeing the unmade bed and the clothes tossed on the floor. Jeans, a tee along with a skimpy pink lace bra and panties.

He was frozen there, imagining what she'd look like wearing those when he heard her footsteps behind him. And her gasp. She hurried around him, practically knocking him down to scoop up the clothes and toss it all into a laundry basket that was on the floor of the adjoining bathroom.

"I take it the intruder didn't leave those things on the floor," Jace commented.

"No." And he could tell from the dread in her eyes that she didn't like that he'd seen them.

"The CSIs and deputies saw them, too," she grumbled. "Trust me, if I'd known my life was going to Hades in a handbasket, I wouldn't have left my dirty clothes lying around."

For some reason, that made him smile. Of course, his head was still swimming with images of Linnea wearing them, and not wearing anything, so he knew he wasn't thinking straight. If he had been, he wouldn't have asked the next question.

"You wear underwear like that all the time?" he blurted out.

Yeah, definitely a stupid question.

"All the time," Linnea verified, and she flashed him. A quick lift of her scrub top to reveal a swatch of pale blue lace. A bra that barely covered her nipples and left plenty of her breasts exposed. "And yes, the panties match."

She didn't flash those, and the disappointment of missing out on that must have shown in his eyes.

"Why did this have to happen now?" she asked on a huff.

"This?" Jace repeated, though he knew exactly what she meant. He just didn't want to be the one to say it, but when Linnea fanned her hand over first him and then herself, he added, "Oh, *that.*"

"Yes, that," she verified with another huff. "We're in danger. My brother wants us dead. On top of that, you've been shot and are in no shape to do anything about *this* or *that.*"

He smiled again, but it was tinged with a grimace this time. Because he now knew exactly how Linnea looked in that skimpy lacy underwear.

"You kissed me in the hospital," she reminded him. "Why didn't you do that sooner? And no, I don't mean the kiss in the barn. Why didn't you kiss me in those dozen years in between?"

"Gideon," he answered without hesitation. "He told me you were hands-off. He thought it'd mess with our friendship to have me hit on his kid sister."

She released a low, slow breath. One that made

him notice the rise and fall of her breasts. "That's stupid."

He nodded. "Especially stupid because it turns out that criminal activity messed with our friendship a hell of a lot more than me hitting on you would have."

Linnea gave him a considering stare, her eyes examining him as if she was trying to decide what to do. Jace knew what he wanted to do. He had relived both of those other kisses and wanted the memories of a third one.

Hell, he wanted to have sex with her so that he'd have those memories, too.

Her gaze dropped, over and up, taking him in and still debating what to do. Jace fixed that by brushing his mouth over hers. Oh, and there it was. The heat. It rippled over his skin and made him forget all about danger, pain and gunshot wounds.

Which, of course, was bad.

Thankfully, he didn't have to muster up enough willpower to stop because his phone did that for him. When he saw Crystal's name on the screen, Jace answered it right away.

"Anything wrong?" Jace immediately asked her.

"No," the deputy assured him just as fast. "I'm back in the office, and I thought you'd want to know that Zimmerman didn't get his warrant. Not yet anyway."

Well, that was a plus for Linnea and him, but Jace

figured the ATF agent would continue to push. If he wasn't out to kill Linnea, then Zimmerman was obviously obsessed with taking her into custody.

"There's something else," Crystal went on. "As I was leaving the hospital, one of the nurses told me that Lieutenant Cannon called to check on Linnea and you. They wouldn't give him any info even when he tossed his badge and rank around, so he said he'd be here later this morning, that it was important he talk to you."

"Apparently, I'm a popular guy," Jace muttered. "If he shows up at the office, just tell him I'm on medical leave."

He had no intentions of telling either Bryce or Zimmerman about Gideon's call. Not yet anyway. If they were dirty, they already knew about it. If they were trying to coerce Gideon, then it might spur them to murder him. That meant Jace had no reason to have a conversation with either man.

Jace finished his call with Crystal and turned back to Linnea. This time, he did some steeling up and forced himself not to think of hot underwear, kisses or sex. What they had to do was critical to stay alive, and it started with talking about Gideon.

"We need to work out what we're going to say to Gideon when he calls back," Jace explained, making sure he sounded as serious as this talk was. "We need to convince him to turn himself in. Now, how do we go about doing that?"

"I can tell him I love him." Linnea answered so fast that it was obvious she'd already given this some thought. "I can remind him that I could be killed if he doesn't try to put an end to the threat."

Jace considered that. Nodded. Gideon had loved his sister. Maybe he still did. And maybe they could use that. Of course, it was just as likely that Gideon would try to use Linnea's love for him to gain any ground he thought could be gained.

Jace's phone rang again, but this time he didn't recognize the number. He hit answer and hoped like the devil that it wasn't Zimmerman or Bryce. It wasn't. It was a woman.

"I'm Tammy Wheatly," the woman said. "Are you Sheriff Castillo, the one who's looking for me?"

"I am," Jace verified, and then he immediately asked. "Where are you?"

"I need to talk to Gideon right now," Tammy went on, obviously not answering his question.

Welcome to the club. "About what?" Jace pressed.

The woman let out a hoarse sob. "Tell Gideon that it went wrong. Tell him that he has me, and that he's going to use me to get to Gideon."

"He?" Jace questioned.

"Just tell Gideon what I said," she insisted.

Jace was just as insistent. "Tell me who has you and where you are."

But he was talking to the air because Tammy had already ended the call.

Get up to 4 FREE FABULOUS BOOKS You Love!

To thank you for being a loyal reader we'd like to send you up to 4 FREE BOOKS, absolutely free.

Just write "YES" on the Loyal Reader Voucher and we'll send you up to 4 Free Books and Free Mystery Gifts, altogether worth over $20, as a way of saying thank you for being a loyal reader.

Try **Harlequin® Romantic Suspense** books featuring heart-racing page-turners with unexpected plot twists and irresistible chemistry that will keep you guessing to the very end.

Try **Harlequin Intrigue® Larger-Print** books featuring action-packed stories that will keep you on the edge of your seat. Solve the crime and deliver justice at all costs.

Or **TRY BOTH!**

We are so glad you love the books as much as we do and can't wait to send you great new books.

So don't miss out, return your Loyal Reader Voucher Today!

Pam Powers

LOYAL READER
FREE BOOKS VOUCHER

YES! I Love Reading, please send me up to 4 FREE BOOKS and Free Mystery Gifts from the series I select.

Just write in "YES" on the dotted line below then return this card today and we'll send your free books & gifts asap!

➡ YES ⬅

Which do you prefer?

| ☐ **Harlequin® Romantic Suspense** 240/340 HDL GRHP | ☐ **Harlequin Intrigue® Larger-Print** 199/399 HDL GRHP | ☐ **BOTH** 240/340 & 199/399 HDL GRHZ |

FIRST NAME   LAST NAME

ADDRESS

APT.#   CITY

STATE/PROV.   ZIP/POSTAL CODE

EMAIL ☐ Please check this box if you would like to receive newsletters and promotional emails from Harlequin Enterprises ULC and its affiliates. You can unsubscribe anytime.

HI/HRS-520-LR21

Chapter Ten

With the laptop next to her, Linnea sat on her bed and listened to the water running in the tub in her bathroom. Jace was in there, taking a bath, something that he'd assured her he could do without her help.

But she wasn't so sure.

That was why she kept her ear turned in that direction while she went over the latest info that Glenn had sent to Jace and then Jace had shared with her. Not the actual official reports but rather a sanitized summary that wouldn't technically violate any procedures.

Scanning through the summary, Linnea could see that the deputy hadn't actually given them any new information, but Glenn had certainly been thorough in his follow-ups. He and the other deputies were still working on the traces for the phones that Tammy and Gideon had used, but they hadn't gotten anywhere on that. Nor had there been any sightings of either her brother or the CI. Since it was going on

3 p.m., it meant it was forty hours or so since anyone had laid eyes on Gideon.

In another part of the summary, Glenn had written that no evidence had been recovered from the woods where Jace and she were attacked by the sniper. No footprints, tire tracks or even any spent shell casings.

That was the bad news. However, there was good news, too, and it was in Glenn's next report. Not an official one that would go in the police files but more like a memo to his boss.

According to that memo, Zimmerman still hadn't gotten a warrant to take her into custody. Definitely good, and Linnea thought his chances of carrying through on that particular threat were growing slim. She sure hoped so anyway. There was enough to worry about without the threat of an arrest hanging over her.

She glanced at the bathroom door again when she heard some moving around. From the sound of it, Jace was getting out of the tub. So it'd been a short bath, less than ten minutes, but he had told her that he wasn't a bath sort of guy. He preferred showers, but because of his wound, he'd opted for the tub so his bandage wouldn't get wet.

Since Crystal had dropped by earlier with an overnight bag of clothes and essentials that she'd gotten from Jace's, he would have something clean to change into. If he could actually get into them, that is. Considering she'd had to help him get dressed at the hospital, Linnea waited for him to ask her to do the same now. But nothing. Until she heard a sound that had her getting to her feet.

A moan.

She knew a moan of pain when she heard one. She went straight to the door. It was slightly ajar, something that Jace had insisted on so he'd hear her if she called out to him. Linnea had wanted it open, as well, in case he slipped in the tub. Well, he hadn't slipped, and he'd even managed to get on his jeans, but he was wincing while trying to get on his shirt. At least he'd taken the two over-the-counter pain pills that she'd left out for him.

"What's a four-letter word for as stubborn as a mule? *J-a-c-e*," she spelled out while he scowled at her.

"I can put on my shirt," he insisted.

"Stubborn *J-a-c-e*," she repeated.

Linnea took the shirt from him and couldn't help glancing down at his bare chest. It probably violated personal rules to gawk at him like that, but it was hard to be this close to him and not notice that he was built. Of course, this wasn't the first time she'd been well aware of that.

He didn't balk when she helped him maneuver his arm into the sleeve, and she had to admit that he probably could have done it by himself. He was moving a lot better than he had just hours earlier, and the wincing had been just that one-time deal.

"I don't mind helping you," she pointed out.

When she looked up at him, he was staring at her. "You've undressed and dressed me more than—" He stopped, cursed, shook his head.

Linnea considered how to fill in the blanks on that, and she came up with one pretty fast. "A lover," she supplied. "Though I suspect your lovers only do the undressing part."

Jace didn't disagree with her about that. "Usually that's the way it works," he said. Definitely a drawl. A sexy-as-sin one that made the heat in her body go up some significant notches.

She saw that gleam in his eye spark into a fire, and while Linnea liked both the spark and the fire very much, she felt she had to remind him of something. So she ran her fingers over the edge of his bandage. Because she thought she'd hurt him, she nearly jerked back her hand when a muscle flickered in his jaw.

But it wasn't pain.

Nope.

She got confirmation of that when he leaned in and kissed her.

This was about as personally dangerous as things could get between them. They were alone, their bodies touching, and everything inside her was begging for more. More that she was certain Jace could give her if he hadn't had that gunshot wound. Still, she settled for this. This kiss. The feel of his mouth on hers.

His taste when his tongue skimmed over hers. The man had certainly made an art form out of kissing.

She leaned in closer, careful not to touch his shoulder, but of course, that left room for a lot of other contact. Specifically, the front of his jeans against the front of hers. Each touch lit new fires and fanned the ones that he'd already started with his mouth.

Jace apparently had plans for a lot more fires today because he hooked his good arm around her waist, lowering his hand to her butt, and pulled her even closer. Oh, yes. This was an art form, too.

Her body molded to his, and she got a jolt of pleasure when she felt his erection. Of course, it was going to have to stay in his jeans, but she allowed herself the thrill of thinking how it would be with him. Amazing, she was sure. Heck, he could probably even manage amazing with a bum shoulder.

He pulled back from the kiss but kept the rest of the body contact, and he stared down at her. "You know this is a mistake," Jace said. "Because of the timing," he clarified. "But later, after the investigation is finished, it won't be a mistake. Understand?"

She did indeed, and Linnea nodded. But she couldn't help but think of the reality of that. Their lives had changed. Would never be the same. They'd be able to get past what happened, but there was no doubt a long, hard road ahead of them. Still, it was nice to know that Jace would be at the end of that road.

And they'd have sex.

Linnea had no doubts about that. It would happen. But apparently not now. Even if Jace had continued the kissing and touching, it would have had to stop because someone rang the doorbell.

Just like that, the heat vanished, and Jace scooped up his gun from the counter. "Stay here," he insisted, and he stormed out, looking very much like a gun-slinger about to face a showdown.

Since it was a showdown he might not be physically up to, Linnea followed him. Not to the door, though. She stayed back in the hall and watched him go to the front window. He peered out the edge of the curtain. And cursed. A moment later, she realized the reason for his profanity.

Because it was Zimmerman.

"I know you're in there," Zimmerman called out. "We need to talk."

Jace didn't answer, but he kept his gun ready.

"I'm not here to arrest Linnea or take her into custody," Zimmerman went on after a loud huff. "I just need to show you something. It's about Gideon."

"You're not coming in," Jace told him, "and I'm not going out there. Whatever you have, you can leave at the sheriff's office, and I'll have one of the deputies bring it to me."

Jace moved away from the window, and Linnea suspected he'd done that so that Zimmerman wouldn't be able to pinpoint his location. Though it would be plenty stupid for the agent to start firing at them in broad daylight where any one of her neighbors would see and hear him.

"I want to talk to you about it," Zimmerman argued, "not to one of your deputies."

"That sounds like a personal problem to me. That's the only offer you'll get from me on this." Jace glanced over his shoulder at her. Seeing his narrowed eyes, Linnea stooped down where she wouldn't be an easy target.

"I can't believe you don't want to see what I have about Gideon," Zimmerman went on. "Unless you believe your old friend is innocent."

"It has nothing to do with my old friend, his innocence or guilt," Jace said, and then he moved again to the other side of the door. "You're a risk, Zimmerman, and I've had my fill of risks."

The agent made a sound of outrage. "I'm not dirty like Gideon."

"Then stop pressing to come inside a house where you're not welcome." Jace went to the kitchen window and looked out.

Linnea's stomach clenched because she realized this could all be a ploy by Zimmerman to distract them while someone tried to break in. If that happened, the security alarm would go off.

Unless Zimmerman had somehow managed to disarm it.

"I'll get my gun," she whispered to Jace, and

she hurried back to her bedroom to take it from the closet.

By the time she made it back to the hall, Jace was in the far corner of the living room, glancing out the window at the side yard. He must not have seen any kind of threat because he merely shook his head.

"Zimmerman, how'd you get the copies of this so-called evidence?" Jace threw out there, still moving. This time to the other side of the house.

"I did my job with a thorough investigation," Zimmerman answered, and unlike Jace, he seemed to be staying put.

Jace huffed. "How'd you get it?" he repeated.

Linnea couldn't see Zimmerman's expression, but she doubted he was happy with Jace's refusal to let him in or his cop's tone.

"I heard buzz that Gideon was trying to get statements from CIs," Zimmerman finally snarled. "And from the security guards at the warehouses where the guns and drugs were taken."

Since that jibed with what Gideon had said, Linnea suspected there would have been a least some talk about it. You couldn't stir up that kind of hornet's nest without creating a buzz.

"I've got statements from CIs and the guards at the warehouse," Zimmerman went on. "But they sounded coached. Maybe intimidated. I think Gideon threatened them. Maybe somebody else did threats, too."

That got her complete attention, but Linnea figured Zimmerman was just going to try to tie her to this. To accuse her of cobbling together lies or half-truths to save her brother.

"If Linnea can't hear me, ask her if Gideon ever said anything about his boss being dirty?" Zimmerman pressed.

"No, he didn't," Jace answered for her. "Do you think Lieutenant Cannon is in this with Gideon?"

Zimmerman definitely didn't jump on that particular train. "I don't know. But I don't think Gideon pulled this off alone. Personally, I think he'd turn to family for that kind of help."

And there it was. Zimmerman was back to accusing her of aiding and abetting her brother. Jace must have been as tired of it as she was, because his next huff was considerably louder.

"Leave now, Zimmerman," Jace demanded. "If you want me to see those statements you've got, then take them to the sheriff's office."

Jace moved across the living room to the window that would allow him to see the front yard and the street. Several moments later, she saw him release the breath he'd been holding.

"Zimmerman's going," he relayed to her. But he continued to stand there and watch even after Linnea heard the sound of a car engine and someone, Zimmerman probably, driving away.

"You didn't see anyone else, did you?" she asked.

Again, he shook his head but then stopped. "What the hell?" he mumbled, and Jace braced himself as if preparing for a fight.

Oh, mercy. That caused her heart to jump to her throat. "Did Zimmerman come back?"

"No, it's a woman."

"A woman?" she repeated, but before Linnea could press him for more, she heard someone call out.

"It's me, Tammy," a voice called out. "I got away from him, but I need help. He'll come for me again."

"She's coming on the porch," Jace said, and he hurried to another window to look out. "Her clothes are torn, and she looks like she has injuries. Call Glenn and ask him to get out here. I want an ambulance, too."

Jace tossed her his phone, and she scrolled through to find Glenn's number, all the while asking herself what the heck Tammy was doing here at her house.

"You have to let me in," Tammy insisted, banging on the door now. "I'm hurt, and he'll come after me."

"Who? Gideon?" Jace demanded. "Is he the one coming after you?"

"No, not Gideon. Not Gideon," the woman repeated through her sobs. "Lieutenant Bryce Cannon. He's not just part of this crime scheme. He's the leader of it."

Chapter Eleven

Lieutenant Bryce Cannon.

Jace definitely didn't like the way the man's name kept coming up in connection with Gideon's crimes. And since Gideon seemed to have a partner in those crimes, Jace figured it would have made things easier for him if his boss had been in on it.

"How bad do you think Tammy's hurt?" Linnea asked, and thankfully she hadn't gone to the window or door to see that for herself. She was still in the hall, and her knuckles had gone white because of the hard grip she had on her gun.

"Hard to tell. There are some bruises on her arms and face, and her dress is torn, but I don't see any blood."

However, what Jace did see were tears and plenty of them. The woman had dropped down onto the porch step and was crying with loud, hiccupping sobs. Her gaze fired all around the yard, the nervy gaze of someone ready to jump out of their own skin.

Jace did feel for her and hated to see anyone hurt.

Well, anyone hurt who didn't deserve it. And he wasn't sure yet if Tammy deserved it or if this was all just a scam. Just like he hadn't wanted Zimmerman to come in, though, Jace had no intention of letting her in Tammy, either. Crying was going to be her golden ticket to come inside and try to go after Linnea or him.

He continued to stand by the window, and Jace watched as the cruiser pulled into Linnea's driveway. It hadn't taken Glenn but just a few minutes, and Jace heard the howl of the ambulance sirens right behind him.

"Stay put," Jace warned Tammy when she got up to run. "My deputy will take you to the hospital where you'll be safe." Where she wouldn't be able to attack, either, but Jace didn't spell that out for her.

"He'll come after me," Tammy howled. "Lieutenant Cannon will kill me."

But she didn't run, not even when Glenn approached. However, Tammy did eye the badge with fear and wariness. Jace had no idea if the emotions were real or not. Since the woman had spent some time behind bars, it was possible that she'd learned how to put on a show, one to convince them that she was a woman in danger.

Jace disarmed the security system so he could crack open the door and speak to Glenn. "This is Tammy Wheatly, a possible material witness along with being Gideon's CI and lover. Yeah, you heard that right," Jace added when Glenn raised an eyebrow. "Ride with her to the hospital."

Which he would be able to do very soon because the ambulance pulled to a stop, and two EMTs rushed out.

"Stay with her at all times," Jace continued with his instructions to Glenn. "When Tammy's medically cleared, bring her back to the sheriff's office. I'll use the cruiser to get Linnea and me there, and we'll wait for you. I want to interview Tammy myself."

Glenn gave him another raised eyebrow. "You think that's safe to go into your office?"

"Not especially," Jace muttered.

But after having Zimmerman and Tammy show up, he figured everyone in Texas must know his location. Besides, he really did want to personally do Tammy's interrogation. He was getting bits and pieces from Gideon and Zimmerman, but it was possible that Tammy had the whole picture.

Jace went back in the house, engaged the security and watched as Glenn and the EMTs got Tammy moving. He also tucked his gun away so he could finishing buttoning his shirt. There was still pain every time he moved his left arm, but it was a lot better than it had been that morning. He credited the bath and ibuprofen for that. Linnea, too. Kissing her was darn effective in helping him forget the pain. Then again, kissing her made him forget a lot of things.

Like common sense.

Maybe it wasn't good common sense now to take her away from her house, but he had an uneasy feelings about staying here. If Tammy was some kind of decoy or distraction, Gideon, Bryce or whoever the heck was after them might be gearing up to shoot into the house. Jace was hoping they'd have second or third thoughts about trying something like that at a police station.

Jace looked back at Linnea, who was still in the hall. "Are you ready to go?"

"Yes." She glanced down at her gun. "Should I bring this with me?"

"Please tell me you have a license for that?" he muttered, but then he waved that off. It might be a good deterrent to a sniper if he saw that both Jace and Linnea were armed. "Bring it."

He had a lockbox in his desk, and he could secure it there. Best not to have any civilian weapons in easy reach since they'd be bringing in Tammy. She was officially a person of interest in this tangled mess. For now anyway. But that could change if Jace found a reason to arrest her.

Jace waited until the EMTs, Tammy and Glenn were in the ambulance before he disengaged the security system and got Linnea out to the cruiser as soon as they'd locked up the house. He said a lot of prayers in that short run they made to the vehicle, and the prayers must have worked, because no one fired shots at them.

"You'll question Bryce?" Linnea asked. She still had a tight grip on her gun, and she was keeping watch.

"I will." And that was another reason he wanted to be in his office. He didn't want Bryce inside Linnea's house any more than he wanted Zimmerman in there. But Jace had to talk to the lieutenant, and like with Tammy, he wanted that to be a formal interview.

Jace parked in front of the sheriff's office and glanced around to make sure there weren't any people lurking around whom he didn't know. Main Street looked as it always did this time of day. Traffic was practically nonexistent, and there was a handful of people going in and out of the shops and businesses. Jace certainly didn't get a bad feeling like the one he'd had at Linnea's.

He hurried Linnea inside and took her into his office so he could secure her weapon. "You might as well get comfortable," he told her. "It could be a while before Glenn gets back with Tammy, and I've got to call Bryce."

"I want to hear what he has to say," she insisted, and she sank down into the chair next to his desk.

Jace sat, too, and even though the jostling around was giving him some jabs of pain, he made sure he kept that pain off his face. He didn't want Linnea snarling out any more "four-letter word" jabs.

Putting his phone on speaker, he tried calling Bryce but then cursed when it went straight to voice mail. Jace left a message for the man to call him ASAP, and then he located the directory for San Antonio PD and got the contact info for Bryce's boss. Captain Katelyn O'Malley. Jace didn't get through right away to her, either. He had to work his way through her admin, but the captain finally came on the line.

"Sheriff Castillo," she greeted. "How can I help you?"

"I'm trying to get in touch with Lieutenant Cannon. It's important," Jace emphasized. "Any idea where he is?"

The captain didn't answer right away. "Important?" she questioned. "Is this about Detective Gideon Martell?"

"In a roundabout way."

And Jace, too, paused to figure out how much to tell her. He didn't know Captain O'Malley, but he had heard that she was a good cop. Still, she was a boss, like him, and he understood the need she might have to protect her people. Hopefully, she wouldn't protect someone who'd betrayed his badge.

"There's a CI, Tammy Wheatly, who just showed up in Culver Crossing, and she claims that Bryce is after her, that he took her captive. I don't have a lot of details," Jace quickly added, knowing that the captain would probably have questions, "but I need to speak to Bryce and get his side of this."

"Of course," she said.

Her voice was cop-flat. But Jace suspected there was a whole lot of emotion going on with those two little words. She definitely wouldn't like that she had another officer, especially one with rank, who could be tied to Gideon.

"According to the schedule, Lieutenant Cannon should be in his office," the captain explained after he heard the clicks of a computer keyboard. "I'll track him down and have him contact you after he speaks with me."

Bryce wouldn't care much for being called into the captain's office. Jace didn't like it much, either. He wanted to throw some questions at Bryce and gauge his reaction before the man had time to think about his answers. Still, Jace couldn't exclude the captain or blame her for wanting first crack at one of her men. But Jace doubted Bryce would make a confession just because his boss, or Jace, pushed him on Tammy's allegation.

No.

There was way too much at stake for that, but there was always the possibility that Bryce might let something slip during an interview that would blow this investigation wide open.

"Oh, and Sheriff Castillo?" Captain O'Malley

continued a moment later. "If you'd copy me on the statement from this CI, I'd appreciate it."

Jace assured her that he'd do that and ended the call.

"Bryce won't go on the run like Gideon," Linnea immediately said. "He'll just deny whatever it is that Tammy says he did to her."

He made a sound of agreement and scrubbed his hand over his face. "And there might not be a reason for Bryce to run. He could be innocent, and this could be an attempt for Gideon to get the light off himself by making a fellow cop look dirty."

Linnea nodded. "But it doesn't get the light off him," she muttered.

No, it didn't, and while Jace thought Linnea might be having doubts as to whether or not her brother was guilty, Jace was almost positive that Gideon had not only broken the law, he'd crushed it.

Cursing, Jace got to work. It wouldn't do him any good to sit and stew while he waited to hear from Bryce, so he got started on pulling up the reports that he hadn't had time to study yet. He especially wanted to take a long look at the ones that dealt with the search at Linnea's. However, before he had time to even get started on that, his phone rang.

"It's Glenn," he told Linnea, and he put the call on speaker.

"Thought you'd want to know that the doctor took Tammy in right away for an exam," Glenn said. "But the EMTs told me they don't think her injuries are serious. Just some scrapes and bruises."

"I noticed. Has she said anything?" Jace asked.

"Plenty. In fact, she started talking in the ambulance and didn't hush while we were getting her into ER. Boss, she insists she was held captive in the barn on Linnea's family ranch."

Jace groaned, shook his head. "That's where Gideon wanted us to meet," he reminded Glenn.

"Yep, I thought that was interesting, too. Another interesting thing she had to say was that she didn't actually see Cannon, but that the guy holding her said he worked for him. Oh, and get this. Her captor wore a ski mask the whole time he had her so she didn't actually see his face."

Jace didn't bother to groan this time. It was exactly what he'd expected the woman to say. Maybe it was the truth that her captor had indeed told her Bryce was responsible. However, it was just as possible that Tammy was making all of this up in an attempt to help Gideon.

"There's more," Glenn went on. "Tammy claims she found a nail on the barn floor and jabbed it into this guy's arm. She says that's how she got away from him. But get this—she insists she dropped the nail right outside the barn door and that it's got the guy's blood on it."

Jace jumped right on that. "We need to get somebody out there to find it."

"Already made the call," Glenn assured him. "One of the CSIs was finishing up at Toby's, and I asked her to make a quick run over there."

"Good." Well, it would be if the nail actually existed. It could be part of the hoax. Still, if there was such evidence, it might be exactly what they were looking for. Because a hired thug could maybe lead them to the person who'd orchestrated all of this.

"I'll call you if the CSI finds anything," Glenn continued. "And I'll bring Tammy to your office as soon as the doctor releases her."

Jace ended the call but immediately got an incoming. From Bryce this time.

"What the hell game are you playing, Sheriff?" Bryce demanded the moment he was on the line. Jace didn't have to guess that the man was thoroughly pissed off.

"No game," Jace assured him. "I need to talk to you about Tammy Wheatly. I have her in protective custody, and she's made some, well, disturbing allegations about you."

"Anything she has to say will be lies, and I get called into my captain's office for that?"

"If what Tammy tells us are lies, then you've got nothing to worry about. Your captain will get that. But you need to come to my office right away so I can get an official statement from you."

"Oh, you'll get a statement," Bryce snarled. "I'll bring a lawyer with me, and we'll be there in about two hours. And afterward, I want to interrogate Tammy."

Jace didn't have to think about that. "I can't let you do that." Because if Tammy wasn't lying, then Bryce's mere presence could intimidate her. "But I'm sending a copy of the report to your captain, and I can do the same for you. Of course, that deal is off if you're part of what's going on with Gideon."

"I'm not part of it." There was such anger, and yes, some bitterness that went into that denial.

Jace ended the call and made a mental note to make sure Tammy had no contact with Bryce. They'd have to be under the same roof, but Jace would need one of his deputies to stay in an interview room with Tammy while he was talking to Bryce.

"He'll hold a grudge," Linnea said. There was no anger, just a weary kind of resignation in her voice. "If he's had no part in this, he could try to get back at you."

Jace raised an eyebrow. "Has he done that sort of thing before?"

"He badmouthed me after I stopped seeing him," she readily supplied. "He told people that I led him on, that I was sleeping around while I was seeing him." Linnea stopped, took a breath. "It was petty and mean. It stopped when Gideon told him to knock it off, though. Bryce apologized, telling me that he was just hurt, but I got the feeling that he wouldn't mind seeing me taken down a couple of notches."

Well, hell. That wasn't good, especially since Jace knew for a fact that Linnea wasn't the sort to lead a man on or sleep around.

"If Bryce is involved with these crimes," Jace said, "this could be the motive for why you were set up for Toby's murder. This way, he can get back at you as well as tie up loose ends so he won't end up behind bars."

Her eyes widened, and she groaned softly. "I'd like to think he's not capable of murder, but I thought the same thing about Gideon just a couple of days ago."

Yeah, so had Jace, and that was why he now had a gunshot wound in his shoulder.

He gave Linnea's hand a gentle squeeze and wished it was more. But this wasn't the place for hugs and such, even if they were meant just to comfort.

His phone rang again, and he glanced at the screen. It was Glenn. Jace hoped something hadn't gone wrong at the hospital. "Is everything okay?" he asked his deputy.

"You could say that. The CSI, April Gendry, went straight over to the barn, and within minutes, she'd found a nail by the door, right where Tammy said it would be," Glenn said, his words rushed together in excitement.

Jace was sure he'd get excited, too, depending on the next answer he got from Glenn. "Please tell me there's blood on it."

"Oh, there's blood all right," Glenn verified. "And here's some better news. April has bagged it and is taking it straight to the lab. Boss, we just might have some answers real soon."

Chapter Twelve

Finally. That was the one word that kept running through Linnea's head while she paced across Jace's office. Once they had the blood examined, Jace and she might finally have the evidence to link all these crimes and attacks.

Of course, that finally might lead them right back to Gideon, but at least then she'd know.

Jace clearly wanted to know, as well, because he'd been on the phone with his deputies and the lab since telling her about the bloody nail. From what she could garner from the conversations, it would be processed as soon as the CSI arrived. Since the lab was in San Antonio, that should be any minute now.

Also from what she'd overheard, Glenn had arranged for a CSI team to go to the barn to look for any other evidence. That would take a little longer, but the CSIs would be on scene before nightfall. Then, maybe they could find other things, other little pieces of the person who'd held Tammy there.

Well, if she had indeed been held.

The bloody nail seemed like proof that she was telling the truth, but Linnea had to consider that it might be part of a setup. The trouble with that was the woman wouldn't have been able to gouge Bryce without him knowing, and he likely would have said something about that when he'd spoken with Jace.

Unless…

A sickening thought slammed into her. Was it possible that the blood on the nail belonged to her? That it'd been taken from those paper towels in Gideon's trash. She considered that.

Dismissed it.

She had a solid alibi, since she'd been with Jace for forty hours or so. No way could anyone say she'd held Tammy captive in that barn. But Linnea hoped and prayed this wouldn't come back to her.

Since her nerves were starting to fire on all cylinders, Linnea forced herself to stop pacing and sat back down so she could continue reading the reports of Toby's murder. It was a lot of jargon, but she got through the first couple of pages. Then froze when she saw the attached photo.

Oh, mercy.

It was Toby, and all it took was one glimpse for her to get confirmation that the man had had a very hard death. So much blood, and his lifeless face still carried a mask of pain.

She looked up when she heard Jace sigh, and he obviously didn't have any trouble seeing what had captured her attention. He merely reached down and closed the file. Then he took her by the hand, urging her to her feet. He gave his office door a little kick to close it and pulled her into the crook of his good arm.

Linnea nearly told him this wasn't necessary, that was she fine. But she practically melted against him. "Take a minute," he said, his voice a soothing whisper. "And then we'll go back to your place. This time though, I'll try to figure out a way to keep the visitors at bay."

She lifted her head from the crook of his neck and looked up at him. "But what about Tammy? You want to interview her. And Bryce."

"Tammy had a panic attack, and the doctor gave her a sedative," Jace explained. "He's keeping her in the hospital overnight and said I wouldn't get much from her right now, that he wants me to wait until the morning to talk to her. We'll have the lab test back by then, so the timing could work better anyway."

"Okay," she said. That did make sense. "But what about Bryce?"

Jace suddenly didn't look so calm and comforting. "Bryce's lawyer called and said he can't get here until around seven o'clock. Maybe even later. I rescheduled the interview for tomorrow morning because I don't want us driving back to your place in the dark."

Neither did she. That would give a sniper an even better opportunity to have another go at them.

"Besides, the same applies," Jace went on. "We'll have the lab results, and if the blood doesn't belong to Bryce, then I'll have time to try to connect the person to him. Or to Zimmerman," he added.

She certainly hadn't forgotten about Zimmerman. "Did you see any signs of injury this morning when he was at my house?"

"No, but he could have changed his shirt, and he didn't actually see Tammy, remember? She waited until after he'd left before she came running out."

That was true, and they didn't know specifically when Tammy had "escaped." It could have coincided with Zimmerman leaving to come to her place. Which brought her to something else on her mind.

"How'd Tammy even know to go to my house?" Linnea asked, but the moment she said it, she knew what the obvious answer was. "Gideon."

Jace nodded. "He could have orchestrated her captivity and brought her to Culver Crossing."

She saw the disappointment of that possibility in his eyes. Still, the nail had to mean something. But what that something was, they wouldn't know until they had the results.

Jace brushed a kiss on her forehead, probably because she looked as if she could use a little more TLC. Since she could, she kissed him. Not on the forehead, either, but on the mouth.

And yes, she got that TLC all right.

Along with the inevitable heat that came with

kissing Jace. A distracting heat that shouldn't be happening since they were in his office and one of his deputies could come walking in. Still, she took her time, letting her mouth sink into his. It was a good kind of sinking that left her feeling a whole lot better. Unfortunately, the whole lot better ended pretty fast because his phone rang again.

The heat vanished when he glanced at the Unknown Caller on the screen. Jace did more than ease back then. He stepped away from her, hit the record function and then answered it.

"Jace," Gideon said. "We need to meet. I've got a time and place—"

"Tell me about Tammy," Jace interrupted.

"Tammy?" he repeated, sounding genuinely surprised by the demand. "What do you mean?"

"I mean tell me about the person who kidnapped her and held her captive."

"What?" The time, Gideon seemed shocked, and Linnea wished she could see his face to know if that shock was anywhere near the real deal. "Where is she? Is she okay?"

Those were the right things that someone might ask if they hadn't had a part in this, but Jace clearly had his doubts. He was scowling and shaking his head.

"Tammy's hurt," Jace answered after a long pause. A pause because he was likely trying to figure how much or how little to tell her brother.

"Who did this?" Gideon snapped. "Where is she? I need to talk to her."

Jace homed in on the first question. "I figured you could tell me who kidnapped her."

"I can't. I swear, I can't," Gideon insisted, his voice thick with worry. Or make that fake worry. "Where is she? Is she okay? How bad is she hurt?"

The rapid-fire string of questions made Linnea wonder if Gideon had feelings for the woman. Maybe. They had been lovers after all, and Gideon might not have gotten involved with her solely for her ties to criminals he could use to fence guns and drugs. However, if Tammy had truly been taken captive, it didn't meant Gideon hadn't had a part in it. It was possible that for some reason he'd set up Tammy's kidnapping, which had somehow gone wrong.

Perhaps his partner in crime had turned on him.

"I don't know who did this," Gideon insisted. "But I'll find out."

Jace cursed when Gideon ended the call. "I wanted to keep him on the line longer," Jace grumbled. "Every second of our recorded conversations could end up giving us clues to find him."

"Yes," she agreed. "But he'll call back. He said he had a time and a place for that meeting he wants with you. A meeting that won't happen, right?"

Jace looked at her, their gazes connecting, and she saw something in his eyes that she didn't want to see. "What's a four-letter word for stupid?" she snapped but didn't wait for an answer. "It's *Jace* if you're thinking about trying to use yourself as bait. You're in no shape to go head-to-head with Gideon."

His eyes narrowed a little. "It wouldn't be bait. But if Gideon knows I'll be there, then he'll come. When that happens, I can arrest him and put him in a cage."

Good grief. He was thinking about putting himself in the crosshairs. "Anything Gideon sets up could be a trap. He's a cop, and he would have already thought of the angles. He could set the perfect trap and kill you. Not because killing you would stop him from being charged with a whole host of crimes but because he wants revenge for you trying to arrest him."

She let the silence linger between them to give Jace a moment for that to sink in. It didn't. So Linnea went with her ace in the hole.

"Gideon could use a meeting like that to double back and come after me," she said.

Jace opened his mouth, maybe to argue, but they both knew he couldn't. Linnea truly believed Gideon wanted Jace dead more than her. However, getting to her would in turn draw out Jace. Then Gideon, or whoever was behind this, could kill them both.

The sound of his phone ringing shot through the silence, and Linnea was glad she'd had the chance to lay out her case for refusing the meeting, since she figured that was her brother calling back. But it wasn't.

"Glenn," Jace told her, and he hit Answer and put it on speaker.

"We got a problem," the deputy said. "April Gendry, the CSI who has the bloody nail, just put out a call for help."

"Help?" Jace snapped.

"Yeah." Glenn muttered a profanity. "The dispatcher heard what she's pretty sure were gunshots while April was on the phone asking for backup."

Linnea pressed her hand to her mouth and forced herself to breathe. Oh, mercy. This couldn't be happening.

Jace did some cursing, too. "Where'd she call from?"

"Just outside of Mercy Ridge. April was probably driving toward the interstate."

That made sense, since the CSI would have had to go through the small neighboring town to get to San Antonio.

"Mercy Ridge cops are on the way to the scene," Glenn added a moment later. "But April's not responding. Boss, it doesn't look good."

DOESN'T LOOK GOOD was a massive understatement. Jace had confirmation of that within a few seconds after being on the phone with Sheriff Barrett Logan.

"The CSI is dead," Barrett said.

Jace wished that he hadn't put this particular call on speaker, because Barrett's words caused the color to drain from Linnea's face. She'd already looked shaky after Glenn's heads-up, but she seemed truly distressed now.

"Two gunshot wounds to the head," Barrett continued. "According to your deputy, she was couriering some evidence to the crime lab, but that's missing."

Of course, it was. Maybe it had been taken to cover up whoever had held Tammy captive. But it was just as possible that it had been stolen to make law enforcement believe that was what had happened. Either way, they didn't have the piece of evidence that could have given them some answers.

But they might have another chance at that.

"I'm stretched for manpower right now," Jace told Barrett, "but I'd like to send over one of my deputies to have a look at the scene. Any objections?"

"None. I suspect the ATF will want in on this, too."

They would indeed, and Jace figured Zimmerman was already on his way there. Well, he would be if he was actually investigating this series of crimes instead of just trying to cover up his involvement.

"Deputy Darnell Hough will be there as soon as I can contact him," Jace assured Barrett.

Jace ended the call to contact the reserve deputy. He then exchanged texts with the other reserve deputy, Manuel Rodriguez, and instructed him to go to Linnea's house to do a search to make sure no one had gotten in. Jace didn't want to be surprised by a killer when he took Linnea home.

And home was exactly where she was going.

Jace didn't think she'd have an actual meltdown, but she definitely wasn't steady. Unfortunately, that unsteadiness would probably get worse because Jace didn't have much time to try to give her any reassurance. He had to put some other things in motion fast.

While he kept an eye on Linnea, he called Glenn and instructed him to beef up security for Tammy. If April had been a target, then the CI could be, as well. That meant using the hospital security guard since Jace didn't want Glenn doing bodyguard duty without a backup.

"We can go soon," Jace told Linnea. "We need to wait for Manuel to give us an all clear on the house, and since he's just up the street at the diner, it shouldn't take him long. I also have another call to make, and I don't want to do it in the cruiser." Once he was in the vehicle, he wanted his focus solely on the drive and getting Linnea safely home.

Linnea nodded and sat up straighter in the chair. Probably because she was trying to convince him that she was okay. She failed big-time. She was nowhere near being okay.

He made that call to get an entire CSI team out to the barn at Linnea's family ranch. Jace insisted they get there fast and go over every inch of the place.

And do that while keeping watch for a sniper.

Because anyone who would kill April and steal evidence wouldn't hesitate to make sure nothing incriminating was recovered at the scene.

"I keep thinking I could have done something to stop this," Linnea muttered. She squeezed her eyes shut a moment, and he could see her fighting to keep it together.

Jace wouldn't tell her that he had been thinking the same thing. That he should have done something. He should have anticipated there'd be a problem and had one of his deputies go with April.

But why had there been a problem?

How had the killer known to go after her and get that evidence?

Both were good questions, and while Jace didn't have answers, not yet anyway, he could maybe do something to help Linnea. Maybe it would help him, too.

"The person responsible for April's death is the person who killed her," Jace spelled out. "Not you and not me."

"But Gideon might be, and I maybe could have…" Linnea trailed off and shook her head.

With her gaze locked with his, she stood and went to him. She didn't hesitate. She stepped into the arm that he circled around her.

"After this is over," she said, "I don't want this to be over."

Jace had to smile because he knew exactly what

she meant. "I don't want it to be over, either." He paused and because he wanted to try to get her to smile, too, he added. "What's a four-letter word for this not being over? *Date*," Jace supplied just in case her mind was heading in a different direction.

"A date?" she repeated.

"Dates," he amended. "I want more than one."

Now she did smile, and it was a darn good thing to see. "Who knows, once you're all healed, maybe it could be more than a date."

That was like an invitation to certain parts of his body. Because, yeah, he wanted more than dates. "I'm feeling all healed now," he said, and brushed his mouth over hers.

He kissed her frown. "You're not all healed," she insisted.

Jace might have kissed her again to prove her wrong. Or rather to try to prove her wrong. But his phone dinged with a text message.

"It's Manuel," he said. "Your house is clear. He'll wait on the front porch for us like he did this morning."

"Are you okay to drive?" Linnea asked.

"Sure." That was his automatic answer, and it was probably true. He could steer with his good arm, but that would mean he wouldn't be able to keep his hand on his weapon.

"You can drive," he amended. It was another bending of the rules, but Jace figured this was a better-safe-than-sorry kind of deal.

He took a moment to drop another kiss on Linnea's mouth, and then he shifted his brain from her to the trip to her place. Gathering their things, he got Linnea her gun, which she tucked into the backpack. Jace then made a quick stop to let the dispatcher know where he'd be, and he went to the door to look out. He didn't see anything out of the ordinary, so Linnea and he hurried to the cruiser. However, he just put the key in the ignition when his phone rang.

Glenn, again. And Jace braced himself for what would no doubt be more bad news.

"Someone set the barn on fire," Glenn immediately said.

Jace groaned. Yep, definitely bad news. "What happened? Is anyone hurt?"

"Don't know yet. One of the neighbors saw the smoke and called it in. The fire chief just let me know about it because he wasn't sure if you'd be in the office."

"I'm on my way to Linnea's," he said as Linnea started driving. Jace kept watch while he considered something. "The CSI team wouldn't have had time to get there, so they probably weren't caught up in this."

Of course, someone else could have been. Maybe someone else the killer had wanted to eliminate.

"Once I'm at Linnea's, I'll make some calls and see what I can find out. Is Tammy still secure?" Jace asked when Linnea turned onto Bluebonnet Lane.

"She is," Glenn confirmed. "She's out like a light, and the doc says she might be that way for a while."

Good, because it meant the woman wouldn't try to escape or cause trouble. But that thought had barely had time to form in his mind when Jace heard something.

A loud popping noise.

His head whipped up, and he looked for whatever had caused it. And he prayed that it was a car backfiring, even though there weren't any other vehicles around.

"Keep moving," Jace told Linnea when she slowed down so she could glance around.

Linnea pressed the accelerator, but she'd only gone a few more yards when he heard the noise again. Louder, this time. And he had no doubts as to what it was.

Because a bullet slammed into the window.

Right next to Linnea's head.

Jace saw the safety glass crack into a spider's web, but it held in place. The bullet didn't get through. But a second one tore into those cracks, weakening the glass even more.

Cursing, Jace pushed her down, leaning over her to try to protect her. She hit the brakes, causing his arm to slam into the steering wheel. Jace could have sworn he saw stars, and the pain ripped through him. Gulping in some hard breaths, he fought to clear his vision. Fought, too, to figure out where the hell the shooter was.

He got a much better idea of that with the third shot.

It, too, came from the driver's side of the vehicle, and it blasted into the rearview mirror. Again, just inches from where Linnea and he were. But it was still a miss, and the shooter had almost certainly been aiming for the window again.

"Stay down," he told Linnea when she started to get up.

"You're hurting, and I can return fire." And she somehow managed to get her gun from the backpack that was on the seat between them.

Well, she sure as heck didn't sound as rattled as she had been in his office. That would come later, though. He was sure of it, but for now Linnea looked ready to help him fight their way out of there. But Jace wanted to minimize the fight. They were in a residential neighborhood with houses. There could be kids around. Hell, this was a prime situation for a bystander to get killed.

"Just stay down," Jace repeated, "but ease up on the brake. I'll handle the steering wheel, and we can get to your house."

Maybe.

But the next bullet ripped through the window, leaving a fist-sized hole and showering Linnea and him with safety glass.

Jace didn't bother cursing this time or playing into that whole hindsight thing. Determined to stop this SOB, he looked through the front windshield to the area where he was sure the shots were coming from. And he saw something.

Or rather *someone*.

A man wearing a ski mask.

He had on black pants and an unbuttoned, bulky gray shirt, and he was crouched down by the side of a house. The guy was already getting into position to fire again.

Since the windshield was bullet-resistant, it wouldn't do Jace any good to return fire through it, and Linnea was in his way for him to get a good shot through the damaged window. Still, it would have to do.

"Stop the cruiser," Jace snapped, and in the same breath, he lifted his gun. Took aim.

And fired.

Jace saw the man stagger back as if he'd been hit. That was when Jace got a glimpse of what the guy had on beneath that bulky shirt.

A Kevlar vest.

Hell.

The chest shot certainly hadn't killed him. The assailant managed to pull the trigger again, and he got off another bullet. It missed the cruiser, going heaven knew where. Hopefully, not into someone's house.

Jace adjusted again, bracing himself on Linnea's back and shoulder, and fired. It was another chest shot, but this time the guy finally fell.

"Stay in the cruiser," Jace told her, and he spotted someone that he wanted to see. Manuel was running toward them.

"Watch Linnea," Jace ordered the deputy.

"You're not going out there," Linnea insisted, and she tried to hold him back.

"I have to do this. He's not dead," he said, throwing open the door. "He probably just got the breath knocked out of him, and I need to get to him before he tries to fire again."

Jace didn't wait for her to argue with him. Bracing his shooting wrist as best he could, he ran across the street and into the yard. He took aim at the gunman as he approached him.

There was blood on the sleeve and shoulder of his shirt. Blood, too, on the right side of the ski mask. The man was writhing in pain, with his gun only a couple of inches from his body.

"I'm Sheriff Castillo," he snapped, as he kicked the gun away. He also did a quick check to make sure the guy had no other weapons.

None.

With his gun still on the man, Jace studied him. Well, what he could see of him. And he suddenly got a really bad feeling in the pit of his stomach. Already knowing what he would see, Jace reached down and yanked off the ski mask.

Oh, hell.

It was Gideon.

Chapter Thirteen

Linnea sat in the passenger's seat of the cruiser and watched as the EMTs loaded Gideon into the ambulance. Her stomach was churning, the muscles clenched so tight that she thought she might get sick. Every nerve in her body felt raw and exposed.

Her brother had just tried to kill her.

There was no doubt about that. She'd seen Jace unmask him. Had seen Gideon fire at the cruiser. Not just once but several times, and his aim hadn't been off. If the glass on the cruiser hadn't been bullet-resistant, Gideon would have no doubt managed to shoot her in the head before Jace pushed her down.

"We'll follow the ambulance to the hospital," Jace said.

Linnea looked over at him as he opened the driver's-side door and raked the safety glass off the seat. Bits of that glass were glistening in his black hair and on his clothes. It was probably the same for her, but Linnea didn't have the energy to do anything about it. Her nerves might have been right at the surface but so was the exhaustion that went all the way to the bone.

"I would ask you if you're okay," Jace said, starting the engine. "But I know you're not."

"Neither are you," she muttered, knowing it was the truth. She could see the weariness in his eyes that was almost certainly showing in hers.

He grunted, possibly agreeing with her, and that was when she saw something else. Jace was keeping watch as they drove to the hospital. Keeping watch in case Gideon had brought his partner or a hired gun with him.

Maybe it was the exhaustion clouding her mind, but having to take such precautions riled her to the core. It wasn't enough that Jace and she had been attacked, again, or that Jace had had to shoot her brother. The danger was still there. And would be until they got answers to put a stop to it.

She prayed her brother could and would give them those answers.

Jace pulled into the hospital parking lot and parked behind the ambulance. He winced when he got out, and Linnea made a mental note to have his wound checked. Heck, it was possible he'd popped a stitch or two. Also possible that he'd gotten new injuries from the flying glass and debris. She hadn't been hurt, but she hadn't had to bolt out of the cruiser to stop them from being killed.

The EMTs rushed Gideon out of the ambulance, and Linnea got a better glimpse of him. His eyes were closed, he wasn't moving, but he was breathing.

And bleeding.

There was blood seeping from an open cut on the side of his head. It looked as if he'd been grazed by a bullet. Or maybe more than grazed. It was possible he had a gunshot wound there.

"Kevlar," she muttered when she spotted the vest.

"Yeah." Jace nodded.

She hadn't seen the vest during the gunfight with Jace, but that explained how Gideon had taken shots to the chest and was still alive. And she knew that Gideon owned such a garment because she'd seen it at his house.

The EMTs wheeled Gideon inside, and Jace and she were right behind them. They followed them to an examination room where the nurse, Arlene Halverson, tried to stop them from entering.

"He's my prisoner," Jace stated. "And he'll be charged with Toby's murder and attempted murder of Linnea and me. He's dangerous."

Obviously Jace's warning got through to the woman because Arlene's eyes widened, and she gave a shaky nod. "We'll use the restraints to make sure he doesn't leave the bed."

Arlene proceeded to do that after the EMTs moved Gideon to an exam table. Jace didn't actually go into the room, but he didn't budge out of the doorway, either. That gave Linnea a chance to get a look at Jace's bandage, and he didn't even try to stop her when she undid the top buttons on his shirt.

No blood.

That was somewhat of a miracle, considering all the moving around Jace had done when he was fighting to save their lives.

"I'm not hurting that much," he assured her as he plucked a bit of glass from her hair and flung it into the trash can.

Linnea returned the favor and got several pieces from the collar of his shirt. "But you're hurting," she stated, knowing it was more than *that much*.

"Once Gideon tells us that name of the person he's working with, I'm sure I won't feel any pain at all," he muttered, his attention still on her brother. Jace paused, groaned. "I really didn't think he'd go after you that way. I knew he wanted me dead. But I thought…" He stopped again, and Linnea saw the hard emotions tightening his face.

"You did what you had to do," she assured him, just in case Jace was having any doubts about that.

That brought his gaze directly to hers, eye to eye. "Yeah," was all he said.

She would have tried again to give him whatever reassurance she could, but his phone rang, and she saw Glenn's name on the screen. Jace gave Gideon another glance, maybe to confirm that he was indeed restrained, and he tipped his head for her to follow him several feet away.

"Just heard Linnea and you were here at the hospital," Glenn said. "You really brought in Gideon? That's what one of the nurses told me."

News traveled fast. Not exactly a good thing in this case, and that was probably why Jace moved her behind him. Her brother might be out of commission for the moment, but his partner could come in with guns blazing since Gideon had failed to finish them off.

"Gideon's here in the ER," Jace explained. As he was talking, Dr. Garcia came into the examining room and went straight to Gideon. "He's hurt and doesn't appear to be conscious."

"So he hasn't told you anything," Glenn concluded.

"He tried to kill Linnea and me, so I guess that's the message he wanted to get across." Jace shifted his attention to the waiting area, glancing around. No doubt trying to assess if there was any kind of danger.

"Linnea and I might be here for a while," Jace continued a moment later. "I need you to call and make sure Manuel's secured the crime scene. The shooting happened on Bluebonnet Lane, just about a block up from her place. Also, check and make sure no one was injured. It's possible some of the rounds went into one of the houses."

"I'll get right on that. The security guard is on Tammy's door, so should I go to the scene now?" Glenn asked.

Jace gave that some thought, probably evaluating if that was his best use of resources. After all, Manuel was a reserve deputy, and he would need help.

"Yes," Jace finally answered. "Go and make sure everything is under control, but then come back in case I need to get Linnea out of here."

She definitely didn't like the sound of that because she didn't want to go anywhere with Jace. Or without getting answers from her brother.

"Okay, I'm heading out the side exit now," Glenn continued. "In the meantime, I can give you an update. I just got off the phone with the fire chief, and he said from his preliminary exam of the barn, the device that started the fire was on a timer. And there was a camera positioned on a tree limb and facing the barn."

"A camera," Jace and Linnea repeated in unison.

"Yes," Glenn affirmed. "It'll be taken to the lab so they can see if it has prints or if it can be traced to anyone. The chief said the camera didn't have any dust or debris on it so it probably hadn't been there long. I'm guessing Tammy's kidnapper put it there to keep tabs on her."

Since Tammy had escaped—well, unless she'd faked the abduction—that made sense. But something else didn't.

"Tammy said she gouged her captor with the nail and then ran," Linnea said, thinking out loud. "So, why wouldn't he have taken the camera with him before he went in pursuit? Or he might have thought he could get her, bring her back and deal with the camera then."

Jace made a sound of agreement, but she could tell from his expression that there were things about Tammy's kidnapping that didn't make sense to him, either.

"Whoever was watching from that camera," Jace added a moment later, "would have seen April retrieve the bloody nail. That could have been how he knew to go after her."

Mercy. That was true. So did that mean Gideon had been the one to kill April? Or had his partner done that while Gideon went after Tammy? She wished that was something she could ask her brother now. Then again, Gideon probably wasn't just going to volunteer the truth if he had indeed committed murder.

"I'll call you if there are any problems at the scene of the shooting," Glenn said before he ended the call.

Jace put his phone away just as Dr. Garcia stepped outside the room and looked at Jace. "I'll need to shut the door while I examine Gideon. And yes, I understand he's dangerous." He tipped his head to Gideon. "I'll keep the restraints on him."

"Good. What can you tell me about his condition?" Jace asked.

"He's alive but unconscious. He's lost some blood from what appears to be an older injury, maybe a gunshot wound. It was treated but not well. It'll need to be cleaned and stitched. Also, judging from the bruises on his chest, he might have some cracked ribs."

"That's from the impact of the bullets on the Kevlar," Jace explained. "What about the head wound?"

"Looks like a bullet graze to me, but I'll know more once I've had a better look at him and run some tests."

"I want him restrained during the tests," Jace insisted.

The doctor nodded, gave a weary sigh. "If we have to move him around, I'll make sure he can't escape."

"Make sure he doesn't grab whatever he can reach and use it to assault or kill you," Jace countered. "Yes, he's that dangerous," he added when the doctor's eyes widened. "How long will he be unconscious?"

"Don't have the answer to that. Head injuries are tricky, and he could be out for a while."

Jace stared at Gideon. "Is it possible he's faking being unconscious?"

"It's possible but not likely in this case," the doctor answered without hesitation. "He had no reaction when I touched his bruises. Or his eyelashes. An awake patient usually has an involuntarily blink response when the eyelashes are touched," he explained.

"Usually?" Jace pressed.

"*Usually* is as good a guarantee as I can give you," the doctor said on a huff. "Now let me examine him, and I'll be able to give you more." He paused. "Well, I can do that if he's under arrest. I'm walking a fine line with privacy concerns—"

"He's under arrest," Jace confirmed. "I'll Mirandize him and interrogate him the second he's awake."

Jace might have tacked on more instructions, but the sound of the ER doors opening had him pivoting in that direction. He drew his gun, causing her heart to jump to her throat. And she soon saw why he'd done that.

Zimmerman came rushing in.

The agent cursed when he saw Jace's weapon aimed at him. "You can put that away, Sheriff. I've heard you have Gideon, and I'm here to take him into custody."

"Take a number," the doctor grumbled. "He's not going anywhere until I release him." Dr. Garcia went back in the examination room and shut the door.

"What's Gideon's condition?" Zimmerman snapped, turning his attention to Jace. "What has he said?"

"Unknown and nothing," Jace provided, and his tone wasn't especially helpful. "And FYI, he just tried to kill Linnea and me, so he's going to answer to that first before you take him anywhere."

That caused Zimmerman to puff up his chest. "The ATF has jurisdiction."

"For the drugs and illegal weapons," Jace readily admitted, sliding his gun into the back of his jeans. "But this was a personal attack on Linnea and me, and it happened right here in my jurisdiction."

Clearly, that didn't please Zimmerman. His eyes narrowed as he spoke. "Any related crimes will be dealt with by the ATF."

Jace leaned in, so close that he violated the agent's personal space. "Gideon just tried to shoot his sister in the head. He opened fire in a neighborhood where he could and maybe did cause injuries. He's going to answer for that."

The stare-down continued for several long moments before Zimmerman finally looked away.

"What are you doing here anyway?" Jace demanded. "How'd you get here so fast?"

Jace hadn't softened his tone one bit, and that seemed to put Zimmerman's hackles back up. "I was in the area. I heard about the dead CSI, and I was on my way to Linnea's to ask you about it."

"So you were close by when Gideon opened fire on us?" Jace pressed. Still no softening, and in fact, that sounded like an accusation.

Which it was.

Zimmerman was high on their list of suspects as Gideon's partner in crime.

"I was about a mile away," Zimmerman snarled. "And no, I didn't have anything to do with it." He appeared to be gearing up to spew out more of an argument about that, but the sound of running footsteps stopped him.

Both Jace and he turned in the direction of the footsteps just as Tammy barreled out of the hall. Her green hospital gown was fluttering around her. Ditto for her hair, and her feet were bare.

And the security guard was chasing after her.

"Gideon?" the woman called out. "Where are you?"

Tammy bolted toward them but came to a quick stop when she spotted Zimmerman. She actually dropped back a step, allowing the guard to take hold of her arm.

"Sorry, Sheriff," the guard said with his breath gusting. "She got away from me after she heard one of the nurses say that Gideon was in the ER."

Jace gave the guard a look that would have made many people shrivel up. Obviously, he was riled. Along with being curious, too. Linnea hadn't missed the way Tammy had reacted to Zimmerman, and obviously neither had Jace.

"You two know each other?" Jace asked, volleying glances at both Zimmerman and Tammy.

"She's Gideon's CI," Zimmerman quickly volunteered.

"Gideon said I shouldn't trust you," Tammy said just as quickly. "Gideon didn't trust you," she added.

Zimmerman huffed. "He said that because he knew I was going to arrest him for all the crimes he's committed."

Tammy stared at him, every part of her body in a defensive pose now, and she shook her head. "Are you the person who hired that thug to take me?" But she didn't wait for answer. "Did he?" She made her plea to Jace.

Jace only shrugged. "To be determined," he answered, causing the anger to flare in Zimmerman's eyes again.

Just then, she saw Bryce come through the ER doors. Great. With Gideon here, the people who wanted Jace and her dead could be only a few feet away from them.

"I heard Gideon was brought in," Bryce said without greeting. Or without an explanation as to why he was there.

Jace picked right up on that. "I rescheduled the interview with you," he snapped, but Jace was looking at Tammy.

Or, more specifically, at Tammy's reaction.

She'd taken a step back when she spotted Zimmerman, but with Bryce, she actually maneuvered herself behind the guard as if using him for a shield.

"Is this the man who held you captive?" Jace came out and asked Tammy.

The woman cowered behind the guard, peering

out to study Bryce. She stared at him for several long moments before her bottom lip started to tremble. "I don't know. Maybe. The man said he was working for Lieutenant Cannon."

"That's a lie," Bryce snarled. He shifted his attention to Jace. "Obviously, the person who had her lied. Or else she made up the story to try to smear me and take the blame off Gideon."

Since that could be the truth, Jace acknowledged it with a nod. "That's why I need to interview both Tammy and you. So I can get to the bottom of what happened."

"I don't want to be here with him. Gideon?" she called out again. Her voice was a lot softer now, barely a whisper, and there was a plea in it.

"Gideon can't answer you," Jace told the woman. "And even if he could, you're not getting in there to see him. Same goes for you," he told Zimmerman and Bryce. "Don't bother to give me the spiel about you being his boss and therefore you have the right to question him," he went on when Bryce opened his mouth. "Right now, Gideon is my prisoner."

Tammy frantically shook her head. "I need to see Gideon. I need to make sure he's all right."

"He's alive," Jace said while motioning to the guard. "Take her back to her room, and this time, make sure she stays there."

The guard did drag Tammy away while she continued to call out for Gideon. Either the woman was in love with Gideon, or else she was putting on a good act.

Jace didn't say anything else until Tammy and the guard were out of earshot, and then he turned to Zimmerman and Bryce. She figured, from the way Jace paused, that he was trying to decide how much to tell them. Or maybe he was deciding the best way to get them out of there. He moved protectively in front of her again, and he had his right hand tucked behind him so that he'd be able to reach his gun fast.

"Tammy claims she managed to gouge her captor with a nail," Jace finally said. "Would either of you like to show me if you have any injuries on your arms?"

Both men were wearing long-sleeve shirts, and while Bryce had his sleeves rolled up to the elbow, it was still possible the fabric was hiding a wound. A wound that might prove he was dirty.

Linnea didn't have to guess what the men's reactions would be, and she was right. Bryce cursed, and huffing, Zimmerman dismissed Jace's words with the wave his hand.

"I have nothing to prove," Zimmerman insisted.

"Neither do I," Bryce chimed in.

"Well, actually you do." Jace directed his comment to Bryce. "Tammy made the accusation, so I figure you want to clear you name."

"How? By letting you do a body search on me? I don't think so," Bryce quickly added. "And if you try, my lawyer will fight you on this. I'm a cop, a ranked officer," he emphasized. "I won't be treated like this."

The man certainly hit all the notes of someone who'd been wrongfully accused, but Linnea wasn't sure if it was bluster to try to cover up the fact that he was as guilty as sin.

"I have nothing to prove," Zimmerman repeated when Jace shifted his attention back to the agent. "The burden of proof in on you about that, and since you no longer have possession of the so-called weapon that Tammy used to attack her captor, then you're barking up a very wrong tree."

"Maybe." Jace paused again. "But I do have something else. Something else that was found at the barn where Tammy was held."

Linnea went still, but she tried to keep her face blank. Maybe Jace was fishing to see if one of them would mention the camera. Neither man bit, though. But both were glaring and obviously waiting.

"Blood," Jace said. "There were a few drops in the same area where the nail was found. The firemen spotted it and collected it before the fire could bring down the barn. This time, I have a team taking the blood to an undisclosed location."

She moved to Jace's side and saw him smile. It was sly and a little mean. The kind of smile that said, "You're toast."

"Soon," Jace added, his voice a warning, "I believe we'll know if one of you is as dirty as Gideon."

Chapter Fourteen

"You lied to them," Linnea said the moment Jace got her out of the hospital and into the cruiser that Glenn had just dropped off for them. "You lied when you told Zimmerman and Bryce that there were blood drops found at the barn."

Yeah, he had, and Jace would continue to lie if it exposed any dirty dealings.

Even after Zimmerman and Bryce had left, Jace hadn't wanted to fill in Linnea on his "plan" while they'd still been at the hospital. Way too many chances for someone to overhear, and he hadn't wanted the talk to get back to Gideon, Zimmerman, Bryce or even Tammy. However, he had wanted Tammy to hear about the blood at the barn, and that was why Jace had instructed the security guard to tell her.

If Tammy was in on her own kidnapping, she would know it was a lie. And if she'd truly been taken captive, then it might give her some comfort to believe the person responsible could be caught.

"If Zimmerman, Bryce and Tammy are Gideon's partners, then they might try to get someone to the barn," Jace explained to Linnea. "That's why I texted one of the reserve deputies and told him to put up another camera. If anyone goes to that barn, we'll know about it."

That would be the best-case scenario. Well, if Gideon didn't confess, that is. The worst-case scenario would be if this lie backfired and caused Gideon's partner to attack them again.

Yeah, definitely the worst case.

When his lungs began to ache, Jace forced himself to release the breath he'd been holding. He also eased up on the grip he had on the steering wheel of the cruiser. And even though this wasn't the same cruiser that Gideon had shot into, just glancing out the driver's window was a gut-punch reminder of how close Linnea had come to dying. He could still hear the sound of the gunshots. Still see the hole in the glass where the bullet had torn through.

And now they were back, literally at the scene of the crime.

Jace drove past the yard that was now marked off with yellow tape with the warning Do Not Cross. The CSIs were in the spot where Gideon had finally gone down, and they were probably checking for spent shell casings or any other evidence that could be used to build a case against Gideon.

Of course, the biggest piece of that evidence was

that Jace and Linnea had actually witnessed Gideon shooting at them. Maybe soon, Gideon would be able to confess that. After he regained consciousness. Something that Jace had to believe would happen. Officially, though, Gideon was in a coma, and Dr. Garcia had no idea just how long that coma would last.

He drove past the CSIs, past Crystal and Manuel, who were still going door-to-door and talking with Linnea's neighbors. Judging from the cars he spotted in driveways, most of those neighbors were now home. They'd likely rushed in from work, or wherever they'd been, to check on their loved ones and property.

"I don't see any masked bogeymen," Linnea remarked.

She said it almost casually, as if this drive wasn't eating away at her. But he knew it had to be. It certainly was getting to him. Although there was some comfort in knowing that there were plenty of law enforcement people and eyewitnesses around. That would make it harder for a gunman to come after them again.

He hoped.

"I don't see Bryce or Zimmerman, either," she added, her gaze flickering to the rearview mirror.

No, neither did he. But it was possible they were around somewhere, since both men had left the hospital before Linnea and him.

"Zimmerman and Bryce pretty much hightailed it out of the hospital," Linnea continued as Jace pulled into her driveway. "But if one of them is Gideon's partner, they might try to find a way to get to him."

That was also part of the worst-case scenario. Linnea and he stood at least a chance of protecting themselves against an attack. An unconscious Gideon couldn't lift a finger to try to stop a killer. That was why Jace had Deputy Darnell Hough guarding Gideon's room. Jace had also given Darnell an order to call him the moment Gideon woke up.

"I'll keep a deputy inside his room," Jace assured her.

He was stretched for manpower, with the multiple investigations going on, but guarding Gideon wasn't an option. He could be the ultimate loose end for someone looking to silence him permanently.

There was also the problem with Tammy. Jace didn't like the woman being near Gideon, and she'd already proven that she could get away from the security guard. Hopefully, though, Tammy would only be staying overnight in the hospital, and then Jace could get her in for questioning. Depending on how she answered those questions, he'd either arrest her or offer her protection.

Since Crystal had already checked the house to make sure no one had broken in, Jace got Linnea inside, and they immediately locked up. According to the security system panel, all windows and doors were armed. That would give them a warning if there was indeed a break-in, but Jace was praying that whoever wanted them dead was done for at least the day. Linnea was clearly wiped out and needed some time to recover from the adrenaline crash.

He got another reminder of the attack when he saw a piece of glass in her hair. As they'd been doing to each other, he plucked this one out, dropping it on the foyer table. What he didn't do was move away from her. He was battling an adrenaline crash, too, along with nerves that had been scraped raw.

Hell.

He'd nearly lost her today.

Jace didn't speak that thought out loud to her. No need. And maybe she was thinking the same thing about him, because on a heavy sigh, she leaned in and laid her head gently on his uninjured shoulder.

"If someone didn't want us dead," she said, "I'd suggest we have a very strong drink. Maybe a couple of drinks." Linnea paused. "Maybe lots and lots of drinks," she amended.

He wasn't much of a drinker, but Jace agreed. A couple of shots of whiskey might help level him out some.

"Can't risk a buzz right now," she murmured.

Jace agreed with that, too. "You could maybe take a hot bath and then we can eat. I could make you a cup of that hot tea you like."

She looked up at him and frowned. "Tea?"

He shrugged. "It's about the best I can offer you right now. That and one shoulder."

Her mouth twitched a little as if she was about to smile. But the smile didn't come. Instead, with the fatigue of the day on her face, she pressed her hand to his cheek. "The one shoulder sounds good," she said. "What can I offer you?"

Jace didn't think she was talking about hot beverages, but it wasn't an offer of sex, either. More like some hand-holding. Maybe a gentle hug or two combined with a pep talk to try to convince them that they'd get through this. That soon, all would go back to normal.

Except Jace didn't think normal was going to cut it anymore for him.

No.

Going through all of this with Linnea had changed things for good. This wouldn't end with them going their separate ways. He'd kissed her, had her body pressed against his. Had wanted her more than his breath.

Still did.

It was the *want* that had him kissing her, but Linnea must not have seen it coming. She made a quick sound of surprise, a sound that he captured with his mouth as he sank into her. Tasting and upping that *want* to a need.

"You're in no shape for this," she muttered against

his lips. But her voice wasn't a protest. More like a mix of silk and heat.

An invitation.

Or so he thought until she eased back a little and repeated, "You're in no shape for this."

He brushed the front of his jeans against hers to give that heat another bump. It worked. Jace saw the flush form on her cheeks. Heard the shivery breath she released. Her eyelids fluttered down for a moment.

"We could just talk sex," she suggested. "It'd be like phone sex."

Jace gave her a flat look. "And that would take care of this ache I have for you?"

"Probably not." She exhaled another of those breaths, along with a little moan, when he bumped her again. "But it would save your shoulder from hurting."

"My shoulder's fine," he assured her. At the moment, that wasn't a lie. He wasn't feeling any pain whatsoever.

To prove that to her, he kissed her again and started backing her into the living room. They might not be able to have sex the old-fashioned way in a bed, but there were plenty of other ways.

"This'll be better than lots and lots of drinks," he told her.

Since he still wasn't sure he'd convinced her of that, Jace just kept on kissing her. Just kept on moving her toward the sofa. As he lowered his mouth to rain kisses on her neck, he found a spot right below her ear that had her moaning again.

The right kind of moan, too.

Heat was right there, rippling off her skin, and the heat had gone hot by the time they reached the sofa. Jace first put his gun on the coffee table and then shifted so that he sat down first. He pulled her onto his lap. All in all, it was a darn good place for her to be. It didn't put any pressure on his shoulder, and it put them center to center.

Jace kept up the kisses but went lower this time. Down to the base of her throat. Then, lower. He kissed her breasts through her top, but soon that wasn't nearly enough. The top had to go, and with her help, he shucked it off her.

And stopped when he saw the bra.

Oh, man. He was toast. The bra molded against her breasts so that her nipples were peeking up over the tops of the black lace. Yeah, black lace. He hadn't realized he had a weakness for such things, but apparently he did. He didn't even wait to get a taste of that, and he took both that lace and her nipple into his mouth.

Not only did Linnea moan again, she also wiggled closer, pressing the center of her thighs right against his erection. The pleasure shot through him, and he knew this was going to have to move a little faster than he'd planned.

Linnea was on board with the faster because she reached between them and unzipped her jeans. Showing some incredible balance, she managed to lever herself up and shimmy out of her jeans, all without leaving the couch.

Her panties were black lace, too, and the sight of them caused Jace to groan. If he hadn't already been rock-hard, that would have done it.

"You can see right through that lace," he told her. "That's not a complaint."

She smiled, a siren's smile, took his hand and slid it into her panties. Jace had planned on going there anyway, but that sped things up.

He touched her. Watched her. The way her mouth opened. The rise of her chest as her breathing quickened. The wet heat as he stroked her. It didn't take many of those strokes before he felt her muscles respond and contract, and he might have sent her flying right then if she hadn't caught onto his hand to stop him.

"No," she said. "I've fantasized about you for way too long for this to be solo. I want us together on his."

Fantasized, huh? Later, Jace would ask her about that, but for now he apparently had to free himself from his jeans. He didn't have time to figure out the logistics of that because Linnea got started on it. She shoved down his zipper, sliding both his jeans and boxers off his hips and freeing his erection.

She looked down, smiled.

"Oh, yes," she said, her voice low and silky. "You're living up to my fantasy."

Jace hoped like the devil that the living up continued, but he had to steel himself up when Linnea leaned to the side to shimmy out of her panties. He was dead sure the image of her doing that would stay with him for a long, long time. Along with giving him plenty of fantasies of his own.

"Condom," he managed to say just as Linnea was about to get back on his lap. "In my wallet, back pocket."

She went right after it, her hands and movements more than a little frantic now. There was some bumping involved, possibly bumps that involved pain, but Jace was past the point of no return. The moment Linnea retrieved the condom, he opened the packet and got it on. Good thing, too, because Linnea didn't wait even a second before she straddled him again.

And took him inside her.

"I've got this," she assured him.

She did. As if to make sure he didn't move around too much, Linnea anchored one hand on his good shoulder and used her other hand to grip the back of the sofa. And she moved.

Mercy, did she.

Linnea created a slow, deep rhythm. Then, not so slow. Then, fast. And faster. Until his pulse was thick and throbbing. Until there was so much need for her that Jace wasn't sure he'd ever get his fill of her.

Apparently, she had her own need for him because with that quickened pace, he felt her muscles squeeze against his erection. Her fingers dug into the sofa while her hips pumped as if to drain every drop of pleasure from this.

Which she did.

As the climax rippled through her, Jace savored the moment for just a heartbeat before he followed her.

Chapter Fifteen

Linnea was thankful for the slack, sated feeling that came with great sex. Thankful for the great sex, as well. Maybe there'd be plenty more of that in her future, but for now, she was just glad that her brain and nerves weren't on full throttle. She needed the lazy calm even if she knew it was only temporary.

Apparently, Jace was having his own "lazy calm" because he didn't seem in much of a hurry when they'd finally gotten up from the sofa. He'd made a quick stop in the hall bathroom and had come out with his clothes back in place. That had been Linnea's cue to get dressed, as well.

And Jace had watched her do that.

He was especially attentive when she slipped on the bra and panties.

Normally, she would have felt the need to cover all her body flaws, which were plentiful, but it was hard to think of flaws and such when there was a hot cowboy giving her an equally hot look.

She was so having him again—soon.

Judging from the smile he flashed her, he knew exactly what she was thinking and wanted to return the favor.

"Please don't say anything about this feeling weird," she told him. "I mean, because you've always thought of me as Gideon's kid sister."

His smile turned a little sly. "Linnea, I quit thinking of you as a kid more than a decade ago. And no, this doesn't feel weird." He paused, his forehead bunching up as if he was giving it some thought. "It feels—"

His phone rang.

Linnea groaned and wanted to insist that he finish what he'd been about to say. However, when he looked at the screen and muttered, "It's Glenn," she knew he had to take the call. He did and put it on speaker.

"Everything's okay," Glenn said right off, probably because he knew they'd be expecting the worst. "I did just have a run-in with Zimmerman, though. He came to Gideon's room and tried to barge his way in. He left when Crystal showed up to bring me some dinner. It's my guess he didn't want to take on two deputies."

Good. Linnea was glad Zimmerman hadn't gotten in with Gideon, because if the ATF agent was Gideon's partner, he could have tried to kill him. Zimmerman might have risked that with just Glenn, but Crystal was some extra insurance. Of course, that didn't mean Zimmerman wouldn't try again.

"Was Bryce with Zimmerman?" Jace asked.

"No. Haven't seen him. But I do have some news about Gideon. That's why I'm calling. The doc is in there with him now, but Gideon opened his eyes a couple of minutes ago."

Linnea hadn't expected that to hit her like a heavyweight's punch. She wanted her brother to regain consciousness. Wanted him to confess all. But she hadn't steeled herself up enough. Just like that, her "lazy calm" vanished, and she got a full reminder of the danger still facing them.

"Gideon didn't say anything," Glenn continued. "He just moaned and tried to lift his hands. He's still restrained," he quickly added. "That's when I called for the nurse, and she had a doctor come in. They asked me to step out while they examined him."

"Stay right there," Jace instructed. "Do you know the nurse and doctor?"

"I do. It's Dr. Garcia and Ashley Dorman. After Zimmerman tried to get in here, I thought maybe he'd try to send in someone posing as medical staff."

"Zimmerman or Bryce. Or, hell, anybody working with Gideon." There was plenty of frustration now in Jace's voice, and his jaw had gone tight.

"Is Gideon still in the ER, or has he been moved to a room?" Jace asked.

"He's in room 119. It's not far from the nurses' station."

Probably because they'd want to keep an eye on him. But the fact that her brother wasn't in ICU probably meant his condition wasn't that bad.

"Linnea and I are coming back to the hospital," Jace said a moment later. "Tell Dr. Garcia that I'll need to speak to Gideon ASAP."

"Will do. Crystal's back at the office. You want me to have her follow you to the hospital?"

Jace opened his mouth, and Linnea was pretty sure he'd been about to say no. But when he looked at her, he must have changed his mind. "Yeah. I want to leave as soon as she gets here. I don't want to give Gideon any time to try to concoct a story to try to make us think he's not as dirty as I know he is."

"I'll call Crystal now," Glenn said. "Be careful, boss. I don't like that Zimmerman and Bryce are out there."

Neither did she, and she knew Jace felt the same way. But what Jace was lacking was any kind of proof that would get one or both men off the street and behind bars. Maybe Gideon could give them that proof.

Linnea hurried to the bathroom to freshen up, and when she came back into the living room, she saw Jace putting his gun in the waist of his jeans. It sickened her that they had to take such measures just to step out of the house. But being outside could be the opening a sniper needed to fire shots at them.

Jace went to the front window to keep watch, and because she knew it was what he'd want her to do, Linnea stayed back. It was ironic that just minutes earlier, she'd been so happy. So pleased. Now Jace and she were facing reality again.

"I'll talk to Tammy, too, while we're there," he said, keeping his attention on the yard and driveway. "I can also find out from her doctor if her condition is really serious enough for her to stay overnight. If she's not in on this, I want her moved to a safe house."

There was something in his voice, something she couldn't quite put her finger on. "You're worried someone will try to kill Tammy."

"It could happen, but I'm more worried she'll try to kill somebody," Jace clarified. "She doesn't have access to a weapon, but since she got away from her security guard to run to the ER, she might be able to sneak something past him." He dragged in a long breath. "If she has to stay in the hospital, I'm calling the Texas Rangers to assist in guarding her."

That was a good idea, but it tightened her chest to think that Tammy might be a killer. A killer in the very place that Jace and she were about to be. Still, they had to go. They had to talk to Gideon.

"Crystal's here," Jace said.

Jace and she went through the now familiar routine of disengaging and then rearming the security system locks before they hurried out to the cruiser. Crystal was indeed there, also in a cruiser, and she followed them out of Linnea's driveway.

The CSIs were still at work, processing the scene of the shooting, and some of her neighbors were milling around, no doubt trying to find any tidbit or gossip that would let them know what had gone on here today. If the whole story wasn't out yet, it soon would be. There'd likely even be talk about Jace and her spending "so much time" alone in her house.

As a rule, Linnea couldn't bother with that kind of speculation. However, she couldn't stop herself from speculating about Jace.

And no, this doesn't feel weird, he'd said. *It feels—* She thought maybe he'd been about to say something like "good." There was a chance, though, that it had felt wrong. Not at the time they'd been having sex, of course. He'd enjoyed that as much as she had. But he was a cop to the bone, and he was probably thinking how unsafe it was to be so distracted.

And it was.

But so were her feelings for him.

Yes, there were feelings. Deep ones. The attacks and the danger hadn't fueled those feelings, but it had made her see that life was too short, too littered with pitfalls not to go after what she wanted.

"I'm falling in love with you," she blurted out.

Linnea wasn't sure who was more surprised by

her confession—Jace or her. The timing sucked, of course, and she'd just contributed to that whole distraction problem, but life was indeed short. If Jace and she didn't make it through this, then it was something she wanted him to know.

The muscles in his jaw stirred, and he gave her a long glance. "I'm a bad bet right now."

"I'm not exactly a good one," she pointed out. "It's just something I wanted you to know."

Obviously, that didn't please him, because his jaw muscles got even tighter. "We'll talk about this later," he said, pulling into the hospital parking lot.

Yes, they would, but Linnea had a horrible thought. One that clawed away in her belly. The thought that there might not be a later. But no way would she hit Jace with that gloom and doom right now. She simply nodded, tried to give him a reassuring look, and they got out of the cruiser as soon as he'd parked it.

As they'd done on their previous visits, Jace and she scanned the waiting room. No one was there today, and the reception desk had a sign that said Be Back Soon, Please Take a Seat.

They moved past the desk and went straight to the hall where there were about a dozen rooms. Jace spotted the security guard, Melvin Carter, in front of what was no doubt Tammy's room. Unlike some of the other hospital guards, Melvin wasn't past his prime. Jace figured the guy was only in his early forties and was in good shape.

"Make sure she stays put," Jace warned the guard.

Linnea and Jace didn't stop. They continued down the hall, which forked off into two smaller wings, each with only four rooms. They went to 119, where Glenn was standing.

"The doctor and nurse just left," Glenn explained. "Dr. Garcia wouldn't give me an update, though."

"I'll get it from him," Jace muttered, and walked into Gideon's room with Linnea right behind him.

Her brother's eyes were closed, but he looked better than he had when he'd been brought out of the ambulance. There was more color in his face, and his head wound didn't look as serious. There was a gash, but it'd been cleaned and stitched.

"I listened at the door," Glenn told them, "but I didn't hear Gideon say anything. The nurse mentioned that he was still unresponsive. Hope I didn't get you here for nothing."

Jace didn't comment on that. He went to Gideon's bed and stared down at him. "You said you saw him open his eyes?" he asked Glenn.

Glenn nodded, and both Linnea and the deputy also moved closer. She watched Gideon's eyelids, looking for any sign of movement.

And she saw it.

Just a flicker, maybe an involuntary one, but Linnea leaned down and got right in his face. "You tried to kill me," she bit out, feeling the anger snap through her like a bullwhip. "Open your damn eyes and tell me why you did that."

Linnea didn't expect for that to work, and that was why she was shocked when it did.

Gideon opened his eyes slowly. Cautiously. And she saw all those shades of blue. Shades that she knew very well because they were practically a genetic copy of her own. Ditto for his hair color, but hers had caught a lot more sun and had streaks that his didn't.

Her brother's gaze landed on her and then immediately shifted to Jace and Glenn. His attention settled on Jace as Glenn stepped out, no doubt to continue guarding the room.

"I need protection," Gideon croaked. His voice was hoarse, and she didn't think he was faking that. "I need a deal."

"You're not getting a deal," Jace informed him, and there was plenty of anger in his tone and expression. "But you are going to tell me who helped you steal and sell guns and drugs."

"I can't." Gideon swallowed hard, cleared his throat and repeated it. "If I tell you, I'm a dead man."

"Why? Who?" Jace demanded.

"I'll be a dead man," Gideon repeated.

Jace glared at him. "If I take my deputy off guard duty, anyone could come in here. Anyone," he emphasized, and it sounded exactly like the threat that it was.

Her brother's eyes widened, and while he might have been shocked that Jace would threaten to do something like that, Gideon seemed to at least consider the possibility.

"I want the name of your partner," Jace insisted. "I want you to tell me about any and every goon who's had a hand in getting your sister nearly killed."

Gideon stayed quiet, but there was plenty going on in his head. Linnea could practically see the fears and thoughts flying around in there.

"I need protection," Gideon insisted. "If you want me to testify, you have to keep me alive."

Jace hesitated, but Linnea figured he would agree to some kind of protection, something he was already providing anyway. But Jace didn't get a chance to voice an agreement because the door opened.

"Boss, we got a problem," Glenn said. And Linnea's heart went to her knees when she saw that he'd already drawn his gun. "A nurse just told me that two armed men came in through the ER. They're headed this way."

JACE FELT THE punch of sickening dread. Hell. He'd brought Linnea here, hoping to get answers, but now he might have put her in another deadly situation.

"Stay back," he told Linnea, and hurried to the doorway, where both Glenn and he scanned the hall.

Nothing.

Not yet anyway. But Jace couldn't see the entire hall. If the gunmen were truly coming from the ER to get to Gideon's room, they'd have to go right past the security guard.

"Call for backup," Jace instructed Glenn. "I want every available deputy up here now, but tell them to approach with caution."

Now probably wouldn't be soon enough, though. The gunmen would have factored that in, that the sheriff's office was just up the street and that Jace would call in backup. That was probably why the thugs intended this strike to be fast, and anyone who got in their way would likely be killed.

"They're coming for me," Gideon snapped. "Get me out of these restraints so I can defend myself."

Jace couldn't do that for the simple reason this could be a ruse to rescue Gideon rather than kill him. If Gideon got free, he might try again to kill Linnea and him.

"This is Sheriff Castillo," Jace called out, ignoring Gideon. "Stay in your rooms and get down. Melvin," he added to the security guard, "you've got armed men coming your way. Get in the room with Tammy and block the door."

Jace had figured his warning would garner some attention. And it did. There were some gasps and screams. The sounds of people scrambling to get out of the path of whatever was coming their way.

Maybe the patients, visitors and medical staff would all stay down. But he'd no sooner had that thought when he heard something else. Not a blast.

But it was gunfire.

Jace was certain of it. It was the swishing sound that came when a bullet was fired through a silencer.

Glenn cursed, obviously knowing exactly what that sound was. Maybe the one that followed, too, because Jace was pretty sure the hard thud was because someone had dropped to the floor.

Someone who'd been shot.

His guess was that it was Melvin. If the guard hadn't managed to get in Tammy's room fast enough, he would have made an easy target. And a necessary one in the eyes of the attackers. No way would they want to leave an armed security guard who could return fire.

There were more screams, and Jace knew some of them were coming from Tammy. "No! No! No!" the woman shouted.

Jace didn't know if the woman was reacting to the guard being shot or if the armed men were now going after her. He couldn't just stand there and let Tammy be killed, but he also couldn't leave Linnea, since the gunmen were almost certainly headed straight for Gideon's room. He had a couple of seconds at most to figure out what to do, and whatever he came up with could have deadly consequences for any one of them.

"Stay here with Gideon," Jace told Glenn. "I'm getting Linnea away from here, and then I'll be back."

Jace didn't give the three of them a chance to tell him what they thought about that plan, but Linnea clearly didn't like it because she started shaking her head. Gideon just kept shouting for Jace to get him out of the restraints.

"Move fast and follow me," Jace said.

He gave Linnea one last glance, hoping to reassure her that he'd do his best to get her out of this. He peeked into the hall, and while he still couldn't see the armed men, he could hear what was no doubt their footsteps. They were indeed heading this way.

The moment Jace had Linnea in the hall, he maneuvered her in front of him. Not easily. He had to keep his shooting hand free, which meant he had to take hold of her with his left hand. The pain shot through his shoulder, watering his eyes and nearly knocking the breath out of him. But that didn't stop him. He kept her moving.

They raced past the nurse station. No one was around, but there was a closed door directly behind the desk. Maybe that was where everyone had taken cover. He considered trying to get Linnea in there, too, but that would mean pounding on the door since it was almost certainly locked. That would take time and would alert the gunmen to where they were.

Jace ruled out sending Linnea to the emergency

exit. It would get her out of the hospital, but it was possible there were other thugs waiting in the parking lot. Since she wasn't armed, she'd make an easy target.

"Go in there," Jace insisted.

It was just three doors down from Gideon's, and the room was empty. He practically shoved her inside and turned to run back to Glenn and Gideon.

But it was too late.

The gunmen rounded the corner of the hall. They were dressed all in black and had on ski masks and Kevlar vests. They immediately took aim at him. And fired. The bullet tore a chunk out of the door frame as Jace hurried inside.

A thousand thoughts went through his head. None good. The shooters had obviously seen him and would be coming this way. Well, they wouldn't if they stopped first at Gideon's room. If that happened, they'd try to take out Glenn before they did whatever else they'd come to do.

Backup had to be on the way by now. His deputies wouldn't just come barging in without assessing the situation. An assessment that was necessary, but it would eat up precious seconds. Those were seconds that Linnea and he didn't have.

"Get in the bathroom," Jace whispered to Linnea. That way, there'd be another door and wall between the shooter and her.

But Linnea didn't head there.

Instead, she scurried across the room and latched onto a metal IV pole that she probably intended to use as a weapon. Jace wanted to believe that it wouldn't be necessary, but the bottom line here was a really bad one. If the gunmen got past him, they'd kill Linnea. He doubted the IV pole would do much to stop them, but it was better than nothing.

He cursed himself for getting her into this. Cursed Gideon for starting this whole chain of danger. Later, if there was a later, he could tell Linnea how sorry he was that this was happening. For now, though, he focused all his energy on saving her.

He tipped his head to her, motioning for her to get behind him. Thankfully, she did do that, but he didn't know whether she'd stay put or not.

I'm falling in love with you.

Her words came back to him now, and they were a chilling reminder that she might do anything to try to save him. Anything that would include sacrificing herself. No way would Jace let her do that.

The footsteps in the hall slowed, and Jace risked sneaking a look outside again to pinpoint the gunmen's location. His heart skipped a couple of beats when he saw them outside Gideon's door. The door was still closed, but it wouldn't stay that way for long. Jace knew he had to do something now.

He adjusted his position. Took aim. And he got lucky. Because the men's attention were on Gideon's door and not him. Jace took full advantage of that.

"Drop your weapons," Jace called out, and the moment one of them whirled in his direction, Jace fired. Because of the Kevlar vests, he didn't go for the chest. Jace aimed at the guy's head.

And he didn't miss.

His shot was dead-on. Literally. The gunman dropped like a stone, but before Jace could do the same to his partner, the second gunman got off a shot. It came so close to him that Jace could have sworn he felt the heat from the bullet.

The gunshot slammed into the wall, and the triggerman didn't stop there. He kept firing. Kept coming right at them. He was pinning them down with the gunfire, and Jace knew once he reached the room, he'd be aiming those bullets right at Linnea and him.

Jace steeled himself up for the attack. He gripped his gun. Waiting. Praying.

Behind him, he heard Linnea's breath. It was gusting, and he knew every muscle in her body was tight and primed for a fight for their lives. Any second now, the gunman would come into view, and he'd fire at him, just as Jace had shot the would-be killer. Both of them might end up dying, but at least Linnea would be okay. He hoped so anyway.

Jace heard some moving around, but the footsteps no longer seemed to be coming toward them. That didn't loosen the knot in his stomach because it likely meant the guy was doubling back to go after Glenn and Gideon.

Then again, this could be the gunman's way of trying to lure Jace out.

It wasn't easy, but Jace stayed put. Listening for the sound of Gideon's door being opened. He heard something, but it sure as heck wasn't a door.

It was a scream.

"Let me go," a woman shouted.

Jace didn't think it was Tammy's voice, and a moment later he got confirmation he was right.

"Someone help me," she begged, and he was pretty sure it was Ashley Dorman, one of the nurses.

Moving to the other side of the door frame so he wouldn't be an easy target, Jace peered out and saw the woman. It was Ashley all right, and the armed thug was behind her. He had Ashley in a choke hold, and his gun was pressed to her temple.

The nurse was a good twelve inches shorter than her captor, which meant there was room for a head shot to take the guy out. But for Jace to get that shot, he'd have to come out from cover. That might have to happen if things went downhill fast—and the conditions for that happening were prime.

"Sheriff, it appears you've got a decision to make," the gunman snapped. He sounded tough enough, but there were nerves in his voice. "Come out and bring Linnea with you or this lady dies."

Jace squeezed his eyes shut a moment and cursed.

He'd seen the look of terror on Ashley's face, and even though he hadn't seen the gunman's face, Jace had no doubts that he'd shoot and kill the nurse. Of course, he'd do the same to Linnea and him if he got the chance.

"If you shoot her," Jace said, "you'll lose your shield. Then, I'll kill you just like I did your partner."

Jace was doing more than merely trying to reason with the thug. He was also alerting Glenn to what was going on. The gunman and Ashley were only a few inches from Gideon's door, and if Glenn came out now, he might be able to knock out the guy from behind. It wasn't without risks, but doing nothing was a bigger risk right now, and if they could take him alive, he might bargain to tell them who was behind this.

The guy bobbled a little, shifting his weight from one foot to the other. He was also firing glances all around. Apparently, he didn't have a plan for getting out of this situation without his dead comrade, and if he panicked, he could end up taking out others in an attempt to escape.

Jace looked out again and saw Gideon's door opening. Just a fraction. Glenn was no doubt trying to figure out the best way to take the guy down. Jace could help with that by keeping up a distraction.

"I'll take the nurse's place," Jace told the man. "Her for me."

"It's gotta be both Linnea and you," he fired back.

Jace jumped right on that. "Who gave you that order?"

"Like I'd tell you that," the gunman snarled.

"Well, you should tell me. You're the one taking all the risks here. Not your boss. You're the one who could be killed."

The gunman paused several moments, and he was no doubt thinking that if he talked, he'd soon be dead. But Jace was hoping that talking was exactly what this guy wanted to do if he had the right incentive.

Jace gave this another push. "Maybe we can arrange a deal," he offered. "Your testimony in exchange for a shorter sentence. Maybe even witness protection."

The man's next round of silence was actually a good thing. Maybe, just maybe, he could get through to them, and no one else would die today.

That thought had no sooner crossed his mind when Jace heard more footsteps. Someone was hurrying toward the junction of the hall. Since it could be his deputies, Jace was about to shout out for them to stay back.

But it was too late for that.

Jace saw Zimmerman rounding the corner, fast, and the ATF agent's eyes landed right on the hostage situation. Zimmerman already had his gun drawn. A gun he aimed at the thug.

And before Jace could do anything to stop it, Zimmerman pulled the trigger.

Chapter Sixteen

Linnea had no trouble hearing the gunshot, and it caused her to break into a cold sweat. For one horrifying moment, she thought Jace had been shot. For one horrifying moment her world had stopped.

Still gripping the IV pole, she moved out from behind Jace so she could see if there was any blood on him. It was hard to force herself to focus, to fight through the panic that was clawing through her. But there was no blood. Not on Jace anyway.

She couldn't say the same for the gunman in the hall.

He was in a crumpled heap on the floor, and there was plenty of blood already pooling around him.

Frozen in place, Ashley started screaming, and Linnea couldn't fault her for it. She hadn't actually seen what had gone on, but she'd figured it out from Jace's and the gunman's brief conversation. The gunman had taken Ashley hostage to try to bargain an exchange.

Ashley for Jace and her.

But it obviously hadn't worked, and the gunman had been shot. Not by Jace, though. Linnea was certain of that. She shifted her gaze to the other end of the hall and spotted Zimmerman. His attention was fixed on the dead guy, a guy he'd obviously just shot, and the ATF agent slowly lowered his gun to his side.

Ashley finally managed to get herself moving, and with her breath wheezing out in panic and fear, she ran to the nurse's station door and started pounding on it with her fist.

And then the chaos started.

Glenn bolted from Gideon's room and took aim at Zimmerman. So did the deputies, three of them, who came barreling around the corner. Their guns were ready, too, and with all the firearms aimed at him, Zimmerman stopped.

"Call off your men," Zimmerman warned Jace.

"I'll call them off when and if I'm sure you're not a threat," Jace shot back.

"I'm not a threat." Zimmerman's voice was as hard and cold as his eyes. "I just stopped one. I heard there were gunmen in the hospital. I saw one, one with a hostage, and I took care of it."

Jace was just as quick to respond. "Maybe you took care of silencing a hired gun who could have ID'd you as his boss."

Zimmerman cursed, and with his glare on Jace,

he lifted his hands and walked toward them. "I saved a woman's life."

"If you'd waited just a few more seconds, I could have talked him into giving himself up."

The agent made a sound as if he wasn't buying that. But Linnea did. Jace had indeed been making progress with the gunman, and she believed he could have defused the situation and arrested the man. Maybe Zimmerman had wanted to make sure that didn't happen. Of course, it could be that he'd unknowingly done someone else a favor by offing the guy.

Jace didn't say anything else until he was eye to eye and practically toe to toe with Zimmerman. "I need you to go to the sheriff's office and give a statement about the shooting." Jace tipped his head to Darnell. "Take the agent's weapon into custody. You'll get it back," he quickly added to Zimmerman, "once everything is cleared up and the paperwork is done."

Linnea figured it was standard procedure to confiscate a weapon used in deadly force. That meant Jace would have to do a statement, as well, since she was pretty sure Jace had killed the guy sprawled outside Gideon's room.

Zimmerman tossed another scowl at Jace, but he didn't resist when Darnell took his gun and motioned for him to follow. Linnea probably would have breathed a little easier at having one less threat right there, but her lungs were so tight that breathing any kind of easy wasn't possible.

Oh, mercy.

This had been a bloodbath, and there was no doubt that Jace and she had been the targets. Maybe Gideon, too.

The moment Zimmerman was out of earshot, Glenn finished up with a phone call and then stepped toward Jace and her. "Crime scene unit is on the way. I told them to expect to be here for a while."

Oh, yes. Two dead bodies. Or maybe more. Linnea remembered the other shot she'd heard.

"What about the security guard outside Tammy's room?" Linnea asked, and she could tell from the way Crystal shook her head that it wasn't good news.

"He's alive, but it looks like he's lost a lot of blood," the deputy explained.

Yes, definitely not good, but at least he was alive.

"Manuel's on Tammy's door," Crystal went on, talking to Jace now. "Not sure we can spare him there for long, though. We'll need to take a lot of statements."

Jace nodded and blew out his breath as if to clear his head. "I need you to guard Gideon." He shifted his attention to Glenn. "Go ahead and coordinate what else has to be done. Statements and the medical examiner. I also need a sweep of the building to make sure no one else was hurt by any stray shots."

"I'll get right on that," Glenn assured him, and

he moved away to talk to the other deputies. Crystal stepped over the dead guy to go into Gideon's room.

Jace turned, looked at Linnea, his gaze combing over her. He was making sure she wasn't injured. The same thing she was doing to him. They'd come out of this without a scratch. Well, none that showed, anyway. Linnea was certain she had enough to fuel nightmares for the rest of her life.

He surprised her by brushing a kiss on her cheek. "I have to talk to Gideon and Tammy," he said. "The chief of staff, too. I'll have to get patients moved from this part of the hall."

Because this was now a crime scene. She understood that. Understood also that this was just the start of a long ordeal. It would have been easier to swallow if they'd learned the name of the person who'd hired the gunmen, but Zimmerman had made sure that hadn't happened.

"Did you send Zimmerman to the sheriff's office to get him out of here?" she asked.

"In part," Jace admitted. "I wanted him away from you and off the street. He'll be at the office for at least a couple of hours. That'll buy me some time to finish up here and get you back to your house."

Where they wouldn't necessarily be safe. But Linnea didn't say that out loud. No need. But along with the adrenaline and the fear came the anger, too. So strong that it felt as if it might punch right out of her. Their lives had been torn to shreds, and she still didn't know why or who was responsible. But her brother did. In fact, Gideon could have been the one who'd hired these men.

"They didn't go into Gideon's room," she pointed out to Jace.

"No, they didn't." He agreed so fast that he must have already been giving that some thought. "But maybe Gideon told them to make it look as if that's where they were heading."

That was the possibility she'd reached, as well. And it was just as likely that her brother had hired more than these two.

Jace went to the dead man Zimmerman had killed, and he leaned down to lift the ski mask. The blood had spread now, and the sight of it turned her stomach as she got a better look at him. His head was seriously damaged with the gunshot wound, but Linnea could see his features well enough. A wide, cleanly shaved face and a large nose that had probably been broken at least a time or two.

"I don't recognize him," she said, swallowing hard and praying that her stomach settled soon. "Do you?"

Jace shook his head and patted down the man's pockets. "No wallet."

Which meant he had no ID on him. That probably meant they'd have to wait for him to be fingerprinted before they knew who he was. Well, they would unless Gideon could tell them.

Jace used his phone to snap a picture of the dead man, and he moved onto the second one. He also had been killed with a head shot, and this time Linnea had to just stop breathing and choke everything back down so she could force herself to get a glimpse of his face. Again, she didn't recognize him, but he had a teardrop tattoo just below his eye.

"A prison tat?" she asked.

"Probably." As Jace had done with the first man, he went through this one's pockets and came up empty again. He took another picture before he stood.

"I want to talk to Gideon," Linnea insisted, and she headed toward his room.

Jace didn't stop her. In fact, he was right behind her as they threaded their way through cops and the medical staff who'd come out of hiding to try to assist. Crystal reached for her gun when they stepped in, a reminder that everyone was still on edge. That included Gideon.

Gideon wasn't still struggling with the restraints, but his wrists were red. There was also sweat on his forehead. "Who's dead?" he immediately asked, directing his gaze and therefore his question at Jace. "Your deputy won't tell me."

"The gunmen didn't tell me their names before they tried to kill us," Jace said.

His voice sounded calm enough, but it was a dangerous kind of calm. Linnea could practically feel the anger coming off him in hot waves.

Jace went closer to Gideon's bed and used his phone to show him the two pictures he'd just taken. Under normal circumstances, her brother probably had a better than average poker face—he'd been a cop after all—but she saw the recognition in his eyes.

"Who are they?" Jace demanded.

Gideon looked away, and for a moment Linnea thought he might stall. But he didn't. "Silas Beck and Teddy Monroe. They belong to a militia group that bought some of the weapons taken from the storage warehouse."

Linnea mentally replayed each word. Gideon hadn't exactly confessed to stealing those weapons, but at least now they had someone to question. Of course, members of a militia weren't likely to spill all to the cops, but maybe Gideon would do that now.

"Who's your partner?" Linnea demanded. "Who hired these thugs to come after us?"

This time, her brother did hesitate. A long time. "I want a lawyer, and I also want to speak to the Culver Crossing district attorney."

"You want a deal," she grumbled, and she didn't tone down the sarcasm.

Gideon looked her straight in the eyes. "I'm sorry for what happened. I'm sorry," he repeated when she huffed. "If I could go back and…" He stopped, shook his head and shifted his attention back to Jace. "Without a deal, I won't stay alive for long."

Jace glared at him. "And I'm supposed to be concerned about that?"

"You should be, what with that shiny, untarnished badge of yours." There was sarcasm in Gideon's voice, too, and a bitterness that sounded bone-deep. "You'll want to get to the truth, and the only way you'll get that is with the DA figuring out how to keep me safe. Then and only then will you get everything you need to tie all of this up in a neat little bow."

Muscles flickered in Jace's jaw. "You're not just going to walk on this. Even if you didn't actually murder anyone, there's conspiracy-to-murder charges—"

"I know what I'm facing," Gideon snapped. He volleyed glances at both of them. "I want to stay alive to make sure the right people go down with me."

Linnea stared at him, trying to figure out exactly who the right people were. Maybe it was a veiled threat against Jace and her. Or maybe he meant his partner and any other thugs they might have hired as hitmen. She just didn't know, and when Gideon turned his head away, she figured he wasn't going to clarify it.

She was right.

"I'm not saying anything else without a lawyer

and the DA," Gideon insisted. "And you won't press because now that I've played the lawyer card, anything else you try to wheedle out of me could possibly be tainted and you might not be able to use against me in a trial."

Judging from the profanity that Jace muttered, that was true. "He stays in those restraints," Jace told Crystal. "When he tells you the name of the lawyer, make the call for him and hold the phone to his ear."

The deputy nodded and took out her phone. Jace didn't wait around. He put his hand on the small of Linnea's back to get her moving out the door. They stepped around the dead body and headed up the hall, away from the other deputies and the chatter.

"I'm sorry," Jace said as they walked.

While Gideon's apology had riled her, Jace's confused her. "For what?" But she didn't wait for him to answer. "For my brother being a selfish SOB who'd rather save his own skin than give you info that could get us out of harm's way along with putting his partner behind bars?"

There was no humor in his smile. A smile that faded as quickly as it'd come. "For that and for putting you through this."

"Oh, we're doing the hindsight thing now." She managed to sound a lot more flippant than she felt. But there was one thing she knew for certain. "This wasn't your fault. It's the selfish SOB's fault along with anyone else who had a part in this."

Jace gave her no indication that he believed that. However, he did give her hand a gentle squeeze as they approached yet more blood on the floor. This one was outside Tammy's room and had almost certainly come from the security guard who'd been shot.

Manuel was right by the door when they stepped in, and like Crystal, he also went for his gun. But he visibly relaxed when he saw Jace. Nothing, however, was relaxed about Tammy. She was huddled in the corner of the room and was sobbing, her face buried in her hands.

"She's been like that ever since I came in here," Manuel explained.

Tammy looked up, her gaze zooming straight to Jace, and she practically leaped off the floor. "Is Gideon okay? Is he hurt?" The words rushed out.

"He wasn't hurt," Jace assured her.

Her face was red, ravaged by the crying jag, and she shook her head. "I want to see for myself. I have to talk to him."

Jace didn't waste any time responding. "Not going to happen. Gideon's in custody, where he'll stay until he's able to be transported to the jail."

That brought on more tears. "Just tell Gideon I need to see him. He'll figure out a way for that to happen."

Jace's sigh was pure frustration. "He'll be transported to jail," Jace repeated. "Once you've been interviewed and I'm convinced you had no part in the crimes or attacks, then you can make a formal request to see him."

Tammy seemed to skim over the first part of that. The part where she would have to get Jace to believe she was innocent. "Let's do the interview now," she insisted. "Then I can make the request."

"I don't have time for an interview now," Jace informed her, but then he stopped, stared at her. "Unless you can tell me the name of Gideon's partner."

Tammy did more headshaking. More crying. "I don't know. That's the truth," she insisted.

Maybe it was, and maybe these attacks had just left Linnea cynical, but she figured Tammy could easily know more than she was saying. If Gideon had asked the woman to stay quiet about naming his partner, Tammy would.

Jace turned to Manuel. "I need you to go to the ER doors and make sure no one else comes in the hospital. If a patient with an actual emergency tries to get in, call me first to clear it before you let them inside. I'm going to call Sheriff Logan in Mercy Ridge and ask if he can send over some deputies to secure the other entrances and exits."

Manuel nodded, then glanced at Tammy. "What about her?"

Jace didn't respond to Manuel but instead stared at Tammy. "I don't have the manpower right now to make sure you do as you've been told and stay put.

But you will stay put, understand? My advice is for you to get back in bed or wait in the bathroom until someone on the medical staff comes in and moves you to another room."

"But what if someone tries to come in and kill me?" she blurted out.

"I'm going to do my best to make sure that doesn't happen. That's the best assurance I can give you right now," he added when she opened her mouth, no doubt to protest that. "The bed or the bathroom," Jace reminded the woman.

Jace took out his phone as they left a still crying Tammy, and he scrolled through his contacts until he got to Sheriff Logan. He was about to press Call when the sound pierced through the hospital. A pulsing blare of noise.

"It's the fire alarm," Jace said right before Linnea caught a whiff of something.

Smoke.

Chapter Seventeen

Jace's hand froze on his phone. His head whipped up and he caught the scent of smoke. Along with the alarm, that confirmed they had a huge problem. Because no way would he believe this wasn't connected to the attacks that'd just happened.

He allowed himself a split second to curse the fact that he hadn't already gotten Linnea out of there. His chat with Gideon and Tammy could turn out to be a fatal mistake. Later, he'd deal with that and what Linnea would perhaps call hindsight. But he should have realized that Gideon's partner wasn't finished. And wouldn't be finished until all the loose ends were tied off.

Gideon was that loose end.

Jace considered having Linnea wait with Manuel and Tammy, but he didn't want her out of his sight. Besides, Tammy could be a loose end, too, and if he left her there, she could soon have to face another hired killer, one that'd have an easier time going after her without Jace around.

"Come with me," Jace told her, and he hoped like the devil that he didn't regret this.

With Linnea in tow, he started toward Gideon's room.

Unlike the gunfire, the alarms brought patients opening the doors to their rooms to see what was going on. Jace did some checking, as well, and while he did see some thin, ghostlike wisps of smoke floating in the hall, he didn't see any flames. That was good, but there were no guarantees it would stay that way.

It was possible Gideon's partner or another hired thug had actually set a fire, but it was just as likely this was a smoke bomb of some sort. After all, a killer wouldn't want to battle a blaze to get to a target. Just in case he was wrong about that, though, Jace went ahead and put in a 911 call to alert the fire department.

While he tried to keep watch all around them, Linnea went back to the fork of the hall. Just then they heard something else. Not gunfire, thank God. But someone yelling.

"Help me," a man said.

Jace saw the man come staggering through the smoke. And he recognized him. It was Eddie Coltrane, an orderly who worked at the hospital. He was wearing his green scrubs and had his hand clutched to his chest.

A chest now soaked with blood.

"Somebody shot me," Eddie told them, and he tumbled forward, collapsing on the floor.

"I need a doctor or a nurse," Jace called out. "I've got an injured man here."

He didn't race toward Eddie, though that was what his instincts were screaming for him to do. Instead, Jace took Linnea by the arm and put her back in the doorway of Tammy's room.

"Don't let anyone get to her," Jace ordered Manuel. He added a stern look to Linnea to make sure she knew he wanted her to stay put. Jace waited for her to nod, and then he hurried to Eddie.

Cautiously hurried.

Because, after all, this could be a trap. But no one jumped out at him. No one came up the hall with guns blazing.

Jace knelt beside the orderly, took one look at his chest and realized this wasn't a hoax. Eddie truly did have what appeared to be a gunshot wound to the chest.

"Who did this?" Jace asked him.

Eddie groaned in pain and continued to clutch his hands over his injury. "Don't know. Didn't see him. I was in the ER, about to head back here to help, and he shot me from behind."

Hell. The guy could be anywhere by now. Maybe coming this way.

But that didn't make sense.

Well, it didn't unless the attacker thought Eddie had seen something. Something that could point the finger at him. It was just as possible, though, that this shooting was some kind of ploy.

"We're evacuating," someone else called out. "We need to move everyone out of the hospital."

It was Dr. Garcia. The doctor was heading their way, and he sped up when he spotted Eddie. He crouched down next to the man, did a quick assessment and yanked out his phone.

"I need a gurney, stat," the doctor told the person he'd called. "I'm outside Room 106. Stat," he repeated.

Jace glanced around, trying to figure out what the hell to do. He couldn't just leave the doc and a bleeding patient here on the floor. If a gunman did come through, he'd finish them off. But he also needed to get to Gideon's room. Because Jace's gut was telling him that Gideon was right now the primary target.

"We're going to have to move Eddie," Jace insisted, and he ignored the doctor's protests while he motioned for Manuel to help him.

Together, Manuel and Jace lifted the man, and Jace got a jolting reminder of his own injury. He must have grunted in pain because Linnea rushed out to help, and together they got Eddie into Tammy's room.

They put him back on the floor, and Dr. Garcia rushed in to continue trying to help him.

"Change of plans," Jace told Manuel. "Stay with Dr. Garcia, Tammy and Eddie. Keep watch because someone armed could try to get up this hall. And alert the fire department that there's another shooter somewhere in the area."

Manuel's nod was a little shaky, but Jace believed the deputy would hold up if there was another attack.

Jace then turned to Linnea. "You can stay here, too—"

"I'm going with you," she insisted, and she took hold of his arm to get him moving.

That meant going back in the hall, and Jace was glad that the smoke was already dissipating. Hopefully, that meant there wasn't actually a fire. But even if there was, the fire department would be there soon, and with Manuel's warning about a possible shooter, maybe they would take precautions. Jace didn't want anyone else shot or dying today.

Especially not Linnea.

He had plenty of doubts about taking her with him, but the doubts would have been even bigger if he'd had to leave her behind. He trusted Manuel and the doctor, but they'd have to evacuate soon, and Jace didn't want Linnea outside unless he was there to help protect her.

Both of them checked over their shoulders as they hurried to the hall junction, and when they turned toward Gideon's room, Jace didn't see the mayhem he'd expected. He'd been gone only about fifteen minutes, but the medical staff had done a good job of clearing out people. Probably evacuating them since he could hear a lot of footsteps heading toward the emergency exit.

The bodies were still there. Not much could be done about them now. Probably on Glenn's orders, the dead guys hadn't even been covered up. That way, the bodies would have less of a chance of picking up stray trace and fibers—something the ME and crime scene folks would appreciate—but it made this trek to Gideon's room even harder. Linnea had seen enough blood and gore, and now she was having to deal with it yet again.

"Maybe they evacuated Gideon, too," Linnea muttered as they approached his room.

She was right, and that caused Jace to curse. Hell, he hoped that hadn't happened, but if it had, Crystal or Glenn would have likely called him. Still, it gave him a bad feeling. A feeling that caused him to position Linnea behind him when he used his forearm to ease open the door.

Jace drew his gun.

However, he'd no sooner done that when the door slammed right into him. Right into his shoulder. The pain knifed through him and nearly brought him to his knees. Worse, it cost him precious seconds. Because whoever had slammed the door into him, threw it open, latched onto Linnea.

And put a gun to her head.

LINNEA HADN'T SEEN it coming. She'd been focused on Jace, on reaching for him to make sure he was okay.

He wasn't.

Neither was she.

She felt the cold hard steel of a gun barrel against her temple and the choke hold of the arm around her throat. Someone had her. Someone who'd already hurt Jace, because she could see that his gunshot wound was bleeding.

Linnea rammed her elbow against the man who was holding her. And it was a man. The muscles in his chest were pressing against her back. He grunted in pain, but his grip only tightened, making it hard for her to breathe.

Jace made a quick move as if he might lunge for her, but her captor only dug the gun in harder. That stopped Jace, and he fired glances around as if looking for help.

But help wasn't there right now.

Crystal was on the floor, and her head was bleeding. Maybe she'd been shot, but Linnea prayed she'd just been knocked unconscious. Probably by the same man who had her now. Either way, the deputy likely wasn't going to just get up and help them.

"Don't kill her," Gideon spat out.

She glanced at her brother, who was still in bed. Still restrained. And he was staring at the man who had her.

"Don't kill her?" her captor repeated. "That's funny coming from you, considering you tried to shoot her."

Oh, mercy. Everything inside Linnea went still. Because she recognized the voice.

Bryce.

Of course, she hadn't forgotten that he was a top suspect, but she hadn't expected for things to come down like this.

"I tried to shoot her because you said if I didn't, you'd do it yourself," Gideon insisted. "And that it wouldn't be *pretty*." Her brother spat out the last word like venom.

"It wouldn't have been. But you failed, Gideon. Your kid sister not only figured out your dirty deeds, she teamed up with the sheriff here to try to stop both of us." *Sheriff* had some venom in it, too. "If I'd left this to you, we'd both either be dead or behind bars—which for cops is the same thing."

It sickened her to think that this had all been because of greedy cops who'd broken the law. And one of those cops was her own brother. Yes, Gideon seemed to be in a bad place right now with his partner, but his own actions had brought him to this.

"Bryce," Jace said. "Let Linnea go. You can't keep killing people to cover up your crimes." Obviously, he was trying to bargain with the man.

"I'm not going to kill you. Not unless I have to," Bryce quickly amended. "But Linnea and you are going to help Gideon and me get out of this mess. We have to go somewhere and lie low for a while. I'm thinking to a country without extradition to the US."

"Help you how?" Jace insisted. He still had a grip on his gun, but he couldn't shoot because she was blocking his line of fire.

"The four of us are leaving," Bryce explained. "We're going to walk out of here, and I'll make sure none of your deputies or Zimmerman gets the chance to shoot me. That's because you'll tell anyone who asks that you and I are transporting Gideon to your office for questioning."

Jace shifted his position and nearly managed to stave off a grimace of pain. Nearly. "No one would believe I'd do that. Gideon is a patient here."

"Then, you'll have to convince them otherwise." Bryce's voice was as calm as a lake. Too calm. And it made Linnea wonder just how many times he'd done something dirty like this. "Remember, all the time you're doing that convincing, I'll have a gun on Linnea."

Bryce lowered his gun to the base of her spine.

"Do anything stupid," Bryce went on, "and I end her with a shot before I turn the gun on Gideon and you."

"And then you'll be arrested," Gideon quickly pointed out.

Bryce made a "yeah, right" sound. "But I won't be dead like you'll be."

"You will," Jace argued. "Because if you fire a shot, then I've got no reason whatsoever to hold back. And I *will* kill you."

Linnea tried to tamp down her pounding heart so she could think. So many things could go wrong in the next couple of minutes, but she had no idea if it was best to try to make a stand here or do that outside. Jace certainly didn't look as if he was in any shape to fight off Bryce, but it might be better than going into the parking lot where plenty of people could be killed if there was a gunfight.

"Jace, take off Gideon's restraints," Bryce ordered. "And remember that part about not doing anything stupid."

Still glaring at Bryce, Jace went to Gideon's bed. Since he could only use his right hand, he had to remove the restraints while also holding on to his gun. Linnea watched as Jace took off Gideon's left restraint, and then he moved to the side of the bed to take off the other one. The moment he'd finished, Jace adjusted his gun so that it was aimed at Bryce again.

"You're going to want to be careful about where you aim that weapon, sheriff," Bryce warned him. "But I'll let you keep it for now. It wouldn't look right if somebody saw you, and you weren't armed."

No, it wouldn't. But if Glenn or maybe one of the other deputies spotted them, they'd still know something was wrong.

She hoped.

"Now, let's move," Bryce ordered. "We'll leave out the side emergency door and go to the cruiser you've got parked by the ER. Another smoke bomb is set to go off right about now. That'll cut down on visibility, so who knows, we might be able just to walk out of here without anyone noticing us."

She couldn't see Bryce's face, but Linnea could see her brother's, and Gideon was scared. She doubted that fear was all for her. No, Gideon probably believed Bryce would murder him as soon as they were out of there.

And she was betting that was exactly what Bryce planned to do.

Along with killing Jace and her. Because Bryce might not have to worry about fleeing or extradition if they were all out of the way.

Her brother got up from his bed. Not easily. Like Jace, he was clearly in pain, and Bryce was well aware of that. Still, she doubted that would stop Jace from trying to fight back if he got the chance.

"Sheriff, open the door," Bryce instructed. "I'll just keep this gun on Linnea's back so you'll make sure to do as you're told."

She saw the debate Jace was having with himself. Their eyes met, and so many things passed between them. Things she wished they'd said. Time that she wished they'd had. But this wasn't over, and Linnea tried to let Jace see that on her face. It wasn't over. She wasn't going to lose him now that they'd finally gotten together.

"There's blood in the hall," she mouthed. "Don't slip on it."

Of course, she meant that for Jace. A way of letting him know that she intended to "slip" once they were out of the room. Bryce might still get the chance to shoot her, but maybe he wouldn't have time to turn the gun on Jace.

Before Jace could even reach for the door, it flew open. He dodged it this time and stepped back before it could smack into him. However, it did hit Linnea, and she staggered back. She felt the gun.

And figured she was a dead woman.

"Gideon!" someone shouted.

Tammy.

She came rushing into the room.

Linnea used the distraction to try to get away from Bryce, but he used his body to knock her to the side so that she landed, hard, on the metal bed rail. The pain shot through, but she tried to jump right back up so she could fight him off.

Fighting him off wasn't necessary, though.

Bryce latched onto Tammy's hair, yanking her back against his chest. Putting the gun to Tammy's head, Bryce muscled Tammy out of the room.

And with Tammy in tow, Bryce started running.

Chapter Eighteen

Jace hurried to the door, ready to go after Bryce, to stop the man from getting away. But if he did that, it would mean leaving Linnea with Gideon. And that was too big a risk to take. He pivoted back.

And his heart dropped.

Gideon had a gun, and he was taking aim at Linnea.

Jace didn't think. He dived at her, catching onto her and dragging her to the floor. Barely in time. The shot that Gideon fired tore into the wall just above their heads.

Gideon walked to the end of his bed. Not easily. He was clearly in pain, gasping and holding his ribs with his left hand. He was trembling, too, but that didn't stop him from pointing the gun at them again.

Jace was dealing with his own pain, and it was crashing into him and robbing him of his breath, but it didn't stop him from aiming, either. He fired, and the shot didn't go into the wall.

It slammed into Gideon's shoulder.

Gideon seemed to freeze, and he looked down at the blood that was spreading across his chest. Directly above the bandage over the other gunshot wound he'd gotten from Jace.

"There was never any evidence to prove I'm innocent. Couldn't be. Because I'm not innocent," Gideon said. His voice was as shaky as the rest of him. "I'm supposed to kill you both, That's why Bryce tucked the gun under my pillow before you came in. I was supposed to kill you both and then escape."

So this had all been a ruse. One meant to eliminate Linnea and him while Bryce and Gideon got away. With no live witnesses, Bryce might not ever get what he had coming to him. And what he had coming to him was justice in the form of the death penalty or life in prison.

"You didn't have to go along with Bryce's plan," Jace pointed out.

"I know." Gideon groaned, repeated it. "But I also knew if I let you live, that you wouldn't stop looking for me. Neither of you would have. You would have just kept hunting until you found me."

Linnea stayed put on the floor behind him, but Jace couldn't risk looking back at her to see how she was handling all of this. But it had to be eating away at her.

Beside them, Crystal started to stir. Jace hoped the deputy was okay, but again, he couldn't check on her right now.

"You're not killing us," Jace warned Gideon. "And you're not escaping. Drop the gun, or I'll put another bullet in you. I'd rather not kill you in front of your sister, but I will if it comes down to us or you."

Gideon's laugh was nearly silent and had no humor in it. "It has come down to me and the two of you." He stopped, groaned and lowered his weapon to his side. "Things got out of hand. I never expected it to go this far."

Jace kept his gun aimed at Gideon, but what he wanted to do was beat him senseless. And go after Bryce and do the same to him. Jace tried not to think of the lieutenant getting away. He'd deal with him later, but for now he had to focus on Gideon. He was no longer pointing a gun at Linnea and him, but Gideon still had hold of it and could decide to use it.

Or rather try to use it.

"You never expected there'd be consequences for murder?" Jace asked, and yeah, there were layers of his own bitterness over what Gideon had done.

"No one was supposed to die. When Bryce first came to me with the plan, it was all about the money. Money we thought we deserved after risking our lives for people who couldn't care less if we died."

So that was the motive, but now it was drenched in bitterness. Stealing goods and cashing them in came with a huge price tag.

"And Zimmerman?" Jace asked. "Was he in on this, too?"

"No. He's clean, but he was sniffing too close to us, so Bryce wanted to set up Linnea to try to get Zimmerman off our trail. I agreed because she knew what I'd done. She knew I was dirty. If I was going to ever have a chance at getting away, then I needed to make sure no one believed her."

That caused the anger to return with a vengeance. "Setting up Linnea for murder," Jace reminded him.

"I didn't kill anyone," Gideon quickly snapped back. "Bryce used his militia contacts to murder Toby and the CSI who was taking in that nail."

And Bryce had done that because he'd thought they were a threat, that they could point the finger at him.

"You tried to murder Jace and me," Linnea reminded him. "You came close to succeeding. I hope it was worth it. I hope all of this was worth it." Her tone was many steps past just being bitter, and Jace couldn't blame her. This was her big brother, someone she'd once loved.

"No. It wasn't worth it," Gideon said.

He let go of the gun, and it clattered to the floor. Still holding his side, Gideon collapsed on the bed. He was bleeding but was still conscious.

Jace and Linnea practically sprang up. But Linnea didn't go to her brother. She helped Crystal up, supporting the deputy's weight and helping her to a chair. Jace hurried to the bed, and even though he doubted Gideon could muster up the strength for a fight, he scooped up his gun, tucking it in the back waistband of his jeans, and he clamped one of the restraints on Gideon's right wrist.

Jace heard the sound of running footsteps, and he cursed when he thought there might be another attack. But it wasn't a gunman who came to the door. It was Glenn. The deputy stepped in and cursed.

"I was coming to tell you that the fire was a false alarm," Glenn said, his gaze firing all around the room. "What the hell happened here?"

"Long story," Jace settled for saying. "Lieutenant Bryce Cannon is behind the attacks, and he just fled the scene, taking Tammy as hostage."

"Tammy," Glenn repeated like profanity. "Zimmerman's here. I just saw him by the back exit. You want me to alert him?"

Jace considered it but then shook his head. The seconds were ticking away much too fast. "Call for a doctor for Gideon and Crystal and stay with them. I'm going after Bryce."

"You're hurt and bleeding," Linnea quickly pointed out. She took Gideon's gun. "I'm going with you."

Jace didn't want to take the time to argue with her. They'd already lost precious seconds, but he didn't stop her from following him when they raced out the door. Jace didn't go toward the back emergency exit but instead went in the direction of the ER.

Linnea and he didn't pass anyone along the way, but Jace could hear the sirens of the fire truck. If the firefighters weren't already in the building, they soon would be.

The moment Jace got to the ER doors, he spotted the cruiser.

And Bryce.

Bryce's back was to them, and he appeared to be trying to pick the lock. Tammy was struggling, obviously trying to get away, but Bryce still had her in a choke hold.

"Drop your gun," Jace ordered, stepping outside.

Bryce went stiff, and Jace could see that the man wasn't going to do that. He pivoted, a movement that caused Tammy to scream even louder.

"I told you he was the one who had me kidnapped," Tammy insisted. "And now he's gonna try to kill me."

Not if Jace had any say in this.

"It's over," Jace told Bryce. "You're a killer, and you'll pay for what you've done."

"It's not over," Bryce snapped. But he was sweating, and his gaze swept all around, obviously looking for an out.

"It is." Jace glanced around, too. He didn't want anyone walking up on this to give Bryce another hostage. "We've pieced it together. You were head of the crime ring that stole those drugs and guns. When things started to go to hell, you did clean up. That included having Tammy kidnapped so you could keep Gideon in line."

That last part had been a theory, but Bryce didn't dispute it. "Gideon's weak. He should have killed you," he repeated.

"But he didn't." Jace went with another theory. "You killed the CSI and stole that nail because the blood on it would have been linked back to you. Not your blood," he clarified. "You wouldn't have done the dirty work of kidnapping Tammy yourself. I suspect that person was either a member of the militia like the hired thugs or maybe one of your CIs."

Bingo. It was the last one, and the anger over his crimes being revealed raged through Bryce's eyes. Yeah, it would have looked plenty suspicious for the lieutenant's CI to be connected to a kidnapping.

The fury continued to build in Bryce, and it came to a head when Bryce yelled, hurling Tammy toward Jace. The woman rammed into his shoulder, causing pain to knife through him. It took Jace precious moments just to get back his breath, and Bryce took full advantage of that.

The dirty cop turned to latch onto Linnea.

But Linnea stopped Bryce in his tracks by bringing up her gun and taking aim at him. "Move and you die," Linnea warned him.

Bryce's breath was gusting, and it seemed as if his every muscle had gone rock-hard. Primed for a fight. But he still had enough restraint left to take a long look at Linnea, no doubt trying to figure out if she would indeed pull the trigger.

She would.

Jace could see that on her face. And Bryce could see it, too.

"Put down your gun," Jace told him.

The moments crawled by, and Jace steeled himself to do what he had to do. Even though she would do it, he didn't want Linnea to take the kill shot. Didn't want her to have to live with that for the rest of her life. She already had enough baggage.

"Gideon should have killed you," Bryce finally said, and tossing his gun aside, he turned toward Jace.

Bryce moved fast. So did his hand as he drew his backup gun from a slide holster in the back of his jeans. Before Jace could fire, the shot blasted through the air. It hadn't come from his gun or the one Linnea had. But from the side.

And it was deadly.

A shot to the head that immediately killed Bryce.

"I heard what the lieutenant said," Zimmerman called out. He came from around the side of the hospital, his gun still aimed at Bryce. "I could see that he was going for his backup."

Jace nodded his thanks, and the agent moved in to help a sobbing Tammy get to her feet. That freed up Linnea to step back, but she didn't waste a second hooking her arm around Jace's waist.

"You're bleeding," she reminded him. "You need to see the doctor right now."

He looked at her to make sure she wasn't in shock. She wasn't. "You're thinking pretty straight, considering you just saw a man gunned down."

"I'll think less straight later when that hits me. For now, I'm getting you back in the hospital."

Jace didn't put up a fight about that. He was indeed bleeding and in pain. But he was feeling other things, too, things that were a lot stronger than the pain. And one of those things was the overwhelming relief that Linnea was all right. Despite all the attacks and the gunfire, she hadn't been hurt.

She led him to an exam room, had him sit on the table and reached into his pocket for his phone. No doubt to call for help. However, before she could do that, Glenn came to the doorway.

"You okay?" he asked Jace right off.

"Yeah." It wasn't a lie. He was a lot better than he had been forty-eight hours ago, when this whole ordeal had started. "Where're Crystal and Gideon?"

"A couple of nurses and Dr. Garcia are with them. Crystal's a little woozy but okay, so I came to check on you. What happened?"

Linnea made that call and requested that a doctor come right away. Jace knew he didn't need immediate attention, but he wouldn't turn it down. Once she'd put down his phone, she started unbuttoning his shirt to get a look at his wound.

"Bryce is dead," Jace explained to Glenn. "He was Gideon's partner."

Glenn nodded as if processing that. "You killed him?"

"No. Zimmerman did. He has Tammy now. How's Gideon?"

"Alive, and Dr. Garcia thinks he'll stay that way. He's got a lot of injuries, but none of them appear to be life-threatening." Glenn paused. "He asked me to tell you that he was sorry."

Linnea's hands froze on his shirt, and she looked up at the deputy. "Sorry," she repeated, but it wasn't with bitterness or sarcasm.

However, there was sadness, and Jace thought that would be with her for a long time. Gideon might be alive, but he would no longer be a regular part of her life. Well, unless she visited him in jail. If she wanted to do that, Jace would support her. Heck, he'd go with her. Anything to ease what Gideon had put her through.

Glenn nodded again and then blew out a long breath. He tipped his head to Jace's bloody shirt. "How bad are you hurt?"

"Not bad." That was the truth, too.

Glenn studied him a moment as if trying to determine if that was true, and then his attention drifted to Linnea. There was something in Glenn's change of expression that had Jace following his gaze.

And that was when Jace saw that there were tears in her eyes.

He sighed, pulled her into his uninjured arm, and glanced at Glenn. "Could you give us a minute? And if the doctor comes, tell him we need a little time to steady ourselves."

"Sure," Glenn said, already closing the door behind him.

Now wasn't the time for a long heart-to-heart talk, something he very much wanted to have with Linnea, but he could try to reassure her that life would get better. He considered how to convince her of that and settled for kissing her.

Linnea responded. First with a soft sound of surprise. Then she sank into the kiss, giving him back everything and more than he was giving her. He'd kissed other women over the years, but nothing was better than being like this with Linnea.

When they were both a little breathless, Jace eased back and checked. No more tears, and some of the sadness was gone, too.

"Mission accomplished," he said. He pushed her hair from her face and left his fingers on her cheek.

"Well, it was accomplished if you meant to make my legs even wobblier and cause my heart to pound really fast."

She took his hand, pressed it to her chest. Yep, her heart was beating hard enough for him to feel it, and he was pleased some of that reaction was because of him instead of the nightmare she'd just been through.

Linnea glanced down at his shoulder. "We really should get the doctor in here to check that."

"I will, but first I need to tell you something." He'd hoped that the words would flow after that opening. They didn't. He mentally hemmed and hawed before he finally said. "You remember when you told me how you felt about me?"

She made a show as if she had to think about that, and even though she'd done that to lighten things up, it sent a pang of fear through him.

"I want you to keep on falling in love with me," he said.

Her eyebrow rose, and despite everything that'd just happened, a smile flirted with her mouth. "I think I can manage that." With that half smile, she kissed him.

And Jace could have sworn his legs got a whole lot wobbly, too.

"I think I can manage even more," she added with her lips still against his.

"Oh yeah? Like what?" He nudged her even closer to him.

"Like…what's a four-letter word for how I feel about you?" she asked.

"Love," he quickly supplied.

She nodded. "Already in love with you."

That unclenched his heart and made him feel a

whole lot better. In fact, it was obviously a cure for his pain.

"That's more than four letters," he pointed out. "But it works for me, too. I'm already in love with you, Linnea."

"Good." Her smile was a lot brighter this time, and it made Jace feel as if everything was truly all right. "Prove it," she challenged.

Jace took her up on that challenge, and he made the next kiss slow, long and deep.

* * * * *

If you missed the previous books in
USA TODAY *bestselling author*
Delores Fossen's
Mercy Ridge Lawmen series, look for:

Her Child to Protect
Safeguarding the Surrogate
Targeting the Deputy

Available now wherever
Harlequin Intrigue books are sold!

WE HOPE YOU ENJOYED
THIS BOOK FROM

HARLEQUIN

INTRIGUE

Seek thrills. Solve crimes. Justice served.

Dive into action-packed stories that will keep you
on the edge of your seat. Solve the crime
and deliver justice at all costs.

6 NEW BOOKS AVAILABLE EVERY MONTH!

#2049 MURDER ON PRESCOTT MOUNTAIN
A Tennessee Cold Case Story by Lena Diaz

Former soldier Grayson Prescott started his cold case firm to bring murderers to justice—specifically the one who destroyed his life. When his obsession intersects with Detective Willow McCray's serial killer investigation, they join forces to stop the mounting danger. Catching the River Road rapist will save the victims...but will it save their future together?

#2050 CONSPIRACY IN THE ROCKIES
Eagle Mountain: Search for Suspects • by Cindi Myers

The grisly death of a prominent rancher stuns a Colorado community and plunges Deputy Chris Delray into a murder investigation. He teams up with Willow Russell, the victim's fiery daughter, to discover her father's enemies. But when Willow becomes a target, Chris suspects her conspiracy theory might be right—and larger than they ever imagined...

#2051 GRAVE DANGER
Defenders of Battle Mountain • by Nichole Severn

When a young woman is discovered buried alive, Colorado ME Dr. Chloe Pascale knows that the relentless serial killer she barely escaped has found her. To stop him, she must trust police chief Weston Ford with her darkest secrets. But getting too close is putting their guarded hearts at risk and leading into an inescapable trap...

#2052 AN OPERATIVE'S LAST STAND
Fugitive Heroes: Topaz Unit • by Juno Rushdan

Barely escaping CIA mercenaries, ex-agent Hunter Wright is after the person who targeted his ops team, Topaz, for treason. Deputy director Kelly Russell is convinced Hunter went rogue. But now she's his only shot at getting the answers they need. Can they trust each other enough to save Topaz—and each other?

#2053 JOHN DOE COLD CASE
A Procedural Crime Story • by Amanda Stevens

The discovery of skeletal remains in a Florida cavern sends cold case detective Eve Jareau on a collision course with her past. Concealing the truth from her boss, police chief Nash Bowden, becomes impossible when the killer, hell-bent on keeping decades-old family secrets hidden, is lying in wait...to bury Eve and Nash alive.

#2054 RESOLUTE JUSTICE
by Leslie Marshman

Between hunting human traffickers and solving her father's murder, Sheriff Cassie Reed has her hands full. So finding charming PI Tyler Bishop's runaway missing niece isn't a priority—especially when he won't stop breaking the rules. But when a leak in her department brings Cassie under suspicion, joining forces with the tantalizing rebel is her only option.